TRUTH IN THE WATER

GINNIE HARPER STATICPUNK MYSTERY
BOOK 2

BRITNEY DEHNERT

Britney Dehnert
BOOKS

For Laurel, who contributed a piece of Felicity's personality when her fun-loving spirit pulled me out of a selfish funk on a sunny, cardboard-riding day;

and for Amanda, whose avid, professional interest in poisons and hazardous materials aided and abetted me in writing this story.

AUTHOR'S NOTE

The staticpunk world is an alternate history world much like cyberpunk or steampunk, where the technology is the focus of contrast between the "punk" world and our own. In staticpunk, the key change is the rise of a fictional apprentice of Nikola Tesla's: Yuri Morislav. His inventions and idealism center on wireless technology that exceed the genius of our own 1890-1930s. We invite you now to this world, a world that looks at electricity and innovation in a completely different way…

In 1890, a young and wealthy manufacturer named Edward Baughmann saw Morislav's potential and invested heavily in him, especially encouraging his inventions that others saw as outlandish or farfetched. Morislav's genius combined with Baughmann's riches and marketing expertise rocketed Morislav's patents into mass production, ushering in an era of technology marked by his ingenuity. Together they built a new production company on the American east coast near Baughmann's hometown, the Park, a quiet village populated mostly by old money. The company attracted workers for miles around, and soon, a large city developed around Morislav Co.

Morislav himself, inspired by the glow surrounding him on the street one foggy night, christened the city Luxity, a city filled with light, and the name took hold. By the 1920s, Morislav is a household name, and his inventions are societal staples.

Ginnie Harper; formerly Eugenia Olivia Candace Harper Elizabeth Jefferson, daughter of wealthy parents from the Park; is a reporter for the *Franklin Journal* in this world.

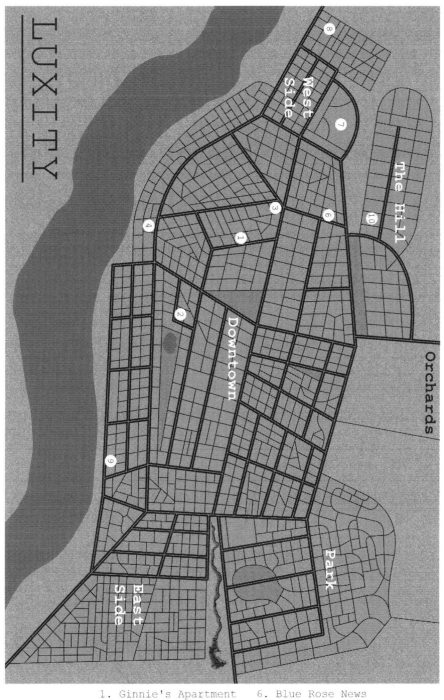

LUXITY

West Side

The Hill

Downtown

Orchards

Park

East Side

1. Ginnie's Apartment
2. Franklin Journal
3. Mel's Diner
4. Sero Electric
5. Panrose Electric
6. Blue Rose News
7. West Hospital
8. Jacobs' Home
9. Devons' Home
10. Chastity's Home

PROLOGUE

S ince the Blaster Murders, I have found that writing a personal account of the more troubling stories I cover enables me to filter and understand what I have seen, heard, and learned. I have not yet encountered a story that wounded me as the Blaster Murders did, but nonetheless, thoroughly recounting each case and story has given me a certain peace of mind.

The newest story I hunted took me down a very odd and twisted path. I believe I will have some difficulty in transcribing this particular case, but I will endeavor to do so in hopes that I may uncover more of the truth that is still hidden to my mind's eye. Unlike the Blaster Murders, this case is not definitively closed. Though Detective Ward has declared it over, I must admit that I am not completely satisfied, and sometimes when we speak of it, I see in his eyes that he is not either. Perhaps we never will be.

1

For me, this story started on my way home from the *Journal*. I had just stopped for a chat with Diggory and his dog, Rufus, sharing the meat pie I'd made the previous night and the apples they'd earned by running errands for the grocer. Rufus appreciated the meat pie, gulping down more than his fair share. While I rebuked Rufus in shocked tones and Diggory snickered at us, a glittering automobile splashed last night's puddle over our lower legs. Sighing at my drenched stockings, I glanced up to see the woman who stepped out of the automobile, and my jaw dropped in a most unladylike fashion.

"Chas?" I said.

The fashionably bobbed head swiveled in my direction.

"Ginnie? I didn't recognize you!" Her manicured hand rested on her heart.

I scrambled to my feet, brushing crumbs from my trousers. A delivery truck zoomed by, splashing across the curb again. "What are you doing here?"

Rufus stood at attention, eying the newcomer with interest, as Diggory jumped up, his head swiveling between us.

"I… I was looking for you, actually," she stammered. "I

had heard that you lived… well, there." She pointed to the apartment building behind us.

"It's good you bumped into me then." I half-smiled. "I live a block from here."

"Oh," she said. Her hand jumped to her pearl necklace.

"Are you headed to a party?"

"After this… errand, yes."

We stood awkwardly for a moment.

Diggory whistled a discordant harmony in that oddly talented way he had, and I jumped a little.

"Pardon me. This is Diggory. And his dog, Rufus, of course." I gestured to the woman. "Diggory, this is my sister, Chastity Jefferson."

"Pleased to make your acquaintance, I'm sure," she said, bending her head delicately.

"Oh me, too," Diggory said with enthusiasm, seizing her hand. "You're a right and proper lady, ain't ya?"

My mouth twitched. "Yes, Diggory, she is. And Diggory is quite the hero, Chas."

"Oh?" Her left eyebrow rose ever so slightly.

"He and Rufus saved my life last February. Perhaps you read about the Blaster Murders?"

She blushed a light pink. "Yes. I read your stories without fail, actually."

I was pleased in spite of myself. "Then you may have read about the murderer's attack on a detective and myself. He was about to finish me off when Rufus and Diggory took him by surprise and chased him into the river."

Diggory swung his arms by his sides. "I dunno as you wouldn'ta got 'im your own self, Miss Harper," he said, modest as any street lad could be. "That little blade was a nice touch."

Chastity blinked at this extraordinary statement and turned to me. "I forget you go by Harper now. Perhaps you've heard that I am no longer a Jefferson either? Though not by the same means, of course."

"You've married?" I asked, taken aback.

She nodded, and her finely penciled eyebrows contracted. "It wasn't in any of the papers, because he's of new money, and, well, Father was not exactly pleased with me marrying someone from the Hill. He was also dead set against having you there, and…" She looked away from me.

I waved away her unspoken apology, feeling stung nonetheless. "I understand. Of course. It was my choice to leave, not yours."

"But to treat you like a *leper*," she said, wrinkling her nose. "Surely that is unnecessary."

I shrugged. "Not to Father, I suppose. But tell me — who is the lucky man?"

Her shoulders squared, the black and silver fabric of her dress shimmering in the noon sun. "Perhaps you remember the Ottisons?"

I nodded. Even poor reporters know the name of the richest steel mogul in Luxity. He was certainly new money — quite a lot of new money.

"Edwin is the eldest son. We were married last spring."

Diggory whistled through his teeth.

"Congratulations," I said, trying to sound hearty and succeeding only in feeling foolish.

The fringe on the bottom of her dress rustled as she studied my face.

"Perhaps we could speak somewhere…"

"Private?" I finished, remembering my manners. "Of course. Please come up for tea. Diggory, thanks for joining me for lunch. The baker promised me a special batch of donuts tomorrow if you'd like to meet me there."

His gossip-hungry face had fallen, but at the sound of such a treat, it lit up again.

"Hot dog! Come on, Rufus! Nice meetin' ya, Miss!"

Rufus gulped the rest of his meat pie, and they raced down the street.

I turned back to my sister, smiling, and saw her dubious expression turn to polite interest.

"Quite an engaging little urchin, isn't he?" she offered.

For just a second, I remembered the heart-pounding moment I knew I would live another day instead of dying at the hands of a murderer — because of the courageous actions of that "engaging little urchin" and his dog.

I sighed. "Quite. Do you want to drive, or shall we walk? It's not far."

Her gaze took in the fallen refuse in front of the next building, the men in jaunty caps whistling and joking across the street, and the little girl making mud pies in the gutter.

"I should see your neighborhood, of course," she said, holding out her hand. I took it with a hidden smile and tucked it in my arm. She smelled of rose water, which immediately took me back to a room papered in violets where she and I stared at the light winking off the cut glass perfume bottles lining Mama's dresser.

"When I'm a lady, I'll always wear rose water," she had declared in her high, childish voice. She was eight at the time.

"You only say that because Lady Eleanor does," I had snipped back, my greater age and experience making me superior.

"And you only say that because you've started French and think you're better than me," she'd returned with her nose in the air. "Anyway, rose water is what all the grand ladies wear, and I am going to be a grand lady someday."

"You!" I'd chortled, looking at her little black ringlets and cherubic face.

Yet here she was, the closest thing to a grand lady that this city could produce, walking arm in arm with me, a working journalist, through the poor lower city and stepping around horse manure.

I shook my head. Times certainly do change, and often not according to one's expectations.

"This is where I live," I said when we reached my apartment building.

"Why, it looks exactly like the other," she declared. "No wonder Jacques was confused."

We mounted the front steps. "What will your driver do while we're inside?" I asked, looking over my shoulder at the car that had slowly followed us. "Shall I ask him in?"

She made a shocked noise. "He'll be fine in the car. My goodness! What an upside down way you live now. Asking the chauffeur inside!" She shook her perfectly groomed head and laughed.

"I daresay he'll get dreadfully hot, Chas," I said. "You have him in quite the suit."

She waved away my comment as I retrieved my key from my vest pocket and inserted it, jiggling the handle to help it unlatch.

"He's used to the heat. Ginnie dear, shall I send him to the bakery for some tea things?"

"Oh, I've got some cookies and even your favorite rose tea," I said. "I don't know why I keep it on hand, to be honest. I never drink it."

"You knew I was meant to visit," she said, smiling at me and removing her gloves as we walked into the shabby three-room apartment.

"Make yourself comfortable," I called, heading to the small corner kitchen to put on the water and take some cookies from the tin on the counter.

"Is this your parlor?" she said humorously, fixing her hair in the mirror across from the rickety table.

"And dining room, kitchen table, and drawing room," I said wryly. "Sit in the chair with the green cushion. The other has quite the personality, and I'm afraid it doesn't behave for visitors."

"So what do you do with yourself when you're not writing about murder and mayhem?" she asked, sitting gingerly in the correct chair and crossing her ankles.

I measured the tea and checked the hissing water. "Not much, I suppose. I've taken to writing an account of the criminal cases I cover, but I've not much of a social life."

She looked sympathetic. "No men chasing you? Your figure is still to die for. I'm desperately jealous."

I shook my head, smiling. "As self-deprecating as always. You look wonderful, Chas."

"So that's a no?" she probed. "Not a single, dastardly handsome man?"

My lips twitched as I thought about my midweekly chats with Thomas Ward. She'd find a detective's friendship about as compelling as a street urchin's. "I look forward to the day when Diggory becomes such an appealing man. For now, I'll have to pine away until he's old enough, I suppose."

A ladylike sigh escaped her tinted lips. She hesitated before she spoke again. "It's Nathaniel, isn't it?"

My chest tightened as it always did when I thought of him. "No. It's not."

Her brown eyes filled with pity. Anger inexplicably rushed over me.

"It's been a long time, Ginnie. Look at your little sister if you don't remember how time passes." She put her chin in her hands and looked reflective. "I could bring you along to some parties, you know." Her eyes were measuring me. "Get you a new dress or two, bob that hair, and I'm sure we could land you a husband with a full bank account and a Ford automobile."

"Not a Morislav Motorcar?" I asked, raising an eyebrow.

She shrugged and sipped at the tea I handed her. "With your stubbornness, I'm sure you could have gotten back into society by now if you'd really wanted to. I'd settle for a Ford man if it's what you wanted."

I chuckled weakly, knowing she was after a laugh. "I've never been one for parties, if you remember. And honestly, I'd rather walk. Fords and MM's snag a bit too much attention around my neighborhood."

She sat back with a sigh. "But that's the whole point, dear. You needn't stay in your neighborhood. A man could make your life easier. You needn't give up your writing either," she added, raising a hand as I opened my mouth. "These are modern times. Why, you could publish books, submit to magazines. No need to scrape a living with that newspaper. You'd have more time on your hands with a servant or two." She glanced at my battered piano-miniature on the table. "You could buy a *real* piano. Don't you miss that?"

I studied her face, feeling protective of my tiny instrument, which I'd played every night since the Blaster Murders: it helped me calm down before bed. Oddly, I'd even taken to tapping out melodies during the day when I was anxious and didn't have it near.

Chastity reached over and poked me. "Ginnie? Yoo-hoo! Don't you miss our Grand piano at home?"

I shrugged and took a bite of cookie, knowing that she was getting at something else. "You have someone specific in mind for this daydream life, don't you?"

When she merely sipped her tea in response, I tapped a rhythm on my knee. "When did you pick up matchmaking? It doesn't become you."

"We'll talk of something else," she said, putting her tea down in a conciliatory gesture.

"Yes, let's. Tell me about your husband. Edwin, was it?"

She nodded and pushed the tea away, lines suddenly appearing on her forehead. "Edwin is a lovely man, but I'm worried about him."

"What?" I asked, startled. "Why?"

Her chair creaked. She fiddled with her cookie. "He's ill. And I don't know what's wrong."

"The doctors don't know?"

She waved a hand impatiently. "They're useless. One knife-happy quack almost removed his appendix. Another said it was ulcers." She shuddered. "Edwin's temper certainly reared its head with that one. The doctor prescribed milk for his stomach through a tube in his nostril."

My hand covered my nose in a reflexive action. She nodded. "It was ghastly. No, the doctors don't know what's wrong." She leaned forward. "Ginnie, I came to you for help."

"What do you mean?"

"People are saying that it's that new hydroelectric generator outside the city, the one that Panrose Electric built. They're saying that it's causing issues with our drinking water. Edwin's not the first one to get sick. Others on the Hill have the same problems: stomach pain, cramps, vomiting, dizziness… horrid stuff."

I rubbed my forehead. "It sounds like a stomach virus. Why would it be the new generator?"

"Remember Gaines? Owner of Sero Electric?"

I nodded. He lived in the Park, near where we grew up.

"He's saying that it can't be a coincidence. He's calling for them to shut the generator down."

"Then why do you need my help?"

"We need the press. Panrose won't do anything about it. They're ignoring us." She paused. "A friend of mine delivered a stillborn child last week. She's been ill with it, too, even before she got pregnant."

I took a deep breath and let it out slowly. "What do you want me to do? I don't write smear stories."

"I understand. But something is better than nothing. Please, Ginnie." She blinked tears from her eyelashes. "I don't know what I'd do without Edwin."

"I'll talk to Mac," I said, picking up my tea. "But why aren't you sick, if it's the water?"

Chastity sniffed. "You know I drink nothing but pure orange juice and champagne."

I raised my eyebrow again and settled back in my chair. "You're drinking tea right now, Chas."

"I stopped when Edwin wouldn't hear of letting our cook go. She makes abominably bitter tea." She took another sip and wiped her eyes, giving me a small smile. "But her leg of lamb is divine. And her cakes. I must have you over, now that we've reconnected."

My eyes twinkled. "But what would I wear?"

"Your birthday's coming up, isn't it?" she said innocently. "Give me your measurements, that's a dear."

2

My mind full of our conversation, I went to Mac the next day to do as I'd promised.

"What? What?" he snapped impatiently. "A new story? What about that story on the mayor's affair? Already done? Fine, fine. It's potentially scandalous? On the electric companies?" His eyes gleamed. "Great, great. Go for it. Take Jacks with you."

"Mac, I really think…"

He waved me out as his phone rang insistently. "No thinking, Harper. Take Jacks and go. I've got a call coming — yes! Mac here! What do you want?"

I backed out and closed his door. Mac had taken to thrusting new assistants on me, hoping for someone to stick. I didn't want a new assistant, but my partially articulated protests landed on deaf ears. Jacks was the greenest one yet. He wasn't a photographer or a journalist or even a tinkerer like Gene had been; he was just a former copywriter from one of the lesser advertising firms in Luxity. I sighed as I walked down to find him.

I was relieved — and slightly aggravated — to find that he

wasn't in, and I headed to my desk to retrieve an autophone. To my surprise, a young woman met me there.

"Felicity Jacks," she said, sticking out her hand. I took it, speechless.

Felicity Jacks was the most uncommon-looking person I had ever met. Her hair was bright orange, her eyes bright blue. Her freckles took over her face and arms (what I could see of them under her plain brown coat), and her nose was long and thin. But what truly impressed the beholder of this unique personage was the mischievous glint in her azure eyes. They were framed by lashes almost ridiculously long, even brushing the top of her eyebrows, and blackened by makeup. With her milky complexion, it was safe to assume that her eyelashes were naturally almost white. The effect of those darting, intelligent, vividly colored eyes with the startling long lashes was one not to be forgotten.

"Hello," I said stupidly.

"You're Ginnie Harper," she supplied for me, smiling coyly. "Mac set me to work with you. He said I'm sixth in a long line since your last assistant kicked the bucket last year."

I winced. "I haven't exactly been counting…"

"Oh, I would if I were you," she said with relish. "It seems such an excellent record. I'm all shivery inside with motivation to do a bang-up job."

"I…" I was at a loss. "I thought Mac had assigned Terry Jacks to me, not… what did you say your name was?"

She threw her head back and laughed. "Terry, Terry. Oh, he'd be hopeless! I'm Felicity, and boy, are you lucky you have me instead of him. He's my cousin, you know. And a complete incompetent. He got me this job, but that's the best thing I can say about him. No, Mac assigned me to you as soon as I got hired —" she flicked her wrist upside down to check her watch — "approximately one hour ago." She grinned at me, and my stomach dropped into my shoes. "This is going to be fun."

Searching desperately for something to say, I tried again. "Your gloves are lovely. I've never felt anything so soft."

She lifted her hand dramatically to her forehead. "Thanks awfully. I worked in a glove factory two jobs before this. Snatched the best ones before I left — paid for them, don't worry." Her eyes twinkled at my expression. "They're cowhide but softened differently than leather. You don't see them much in the lower city."

"Two jobs before this? Where else have you worked?"

"Oh honey, you lost count of your assistants; I lost count of my jobs. We're even." She furrowed her brow and started ticking names off her fingers. "Let's see. I worked for the telegraph company — can't remember the name now — I worked the switchboards at Morislav's 'Phone Company, I was a secretary at the Vangees Company, a laundress at Nelly's Laundry, and a waitress at Delly's Diner. They sound related, don't they? Nelly and Delly? It's such a scream that I worked at both." She laughed delightedly and adjusted the strap of her bright green purse on her shoulder. "I even cleaned for the nuns at that Catholic school on the east end. That's when I took up photography with my dad's camera. They threw me out after a month, but I had a real time of it."

I found myself spellbound — or perhaps dazed. "You're quite the jack-of-all-trades."

She grinned evilly. "And you like your puns. Mac didn't tell me that."

It took me a moment before I realized what she meant. "Oh. Yes. Felicity Jacks. Sorry. So Mac hired you today then? And assigned you to me?" I was still reeling.

She nodded smugly. "Terry told me his boss was a modern newspaper man who did everything his own way, and I should have believed him. I didn't think he'd hire a woman for anything but a secretary, but he sure did, and I'm just as pleased as punch. So where are we off to first? I've got my camera all ready."

She looked at me expectantly, and it finally sunk in to my stunned brain that this extraordinary woman was in my charge now. I took a deep breath.

"Sero Electric." I rummaged for my autophone and an extra pad of paper, trying to organize my thoughts. Once I was satisfied that I'd gathered myself together sufficiently to explain the investigation, I looked up and found that she had already bounded out the door.

I was staring, my mouth slightly open, when another reporter hurried up with a stack of papers in his arms. He gave an admiring whistle and indicated the door with his head.

"How'd you get the new one, Ginnie? Mac should've given her to someone who would appreciate what he's got. Like me, for instance. I s'pose he thought the ladies should stick together, eh?" He gave a despondent shake of his head and left.

I rolled my eyes and hurried to the door. The first day on this story was already more exciting than I had bargained.

"There you are," Felicity said as I caught up to her. She'd been standing, hands on her hips, facing the street a block down from the *Journal*. "Sero Electric is this way, isn't it?" She jabbed to her right with her thumb.

I nodded. "We're going to ask them some questions about the new hydro-electric generator by the Hill. My si—an acquaintance gave me the lead."

"A si—quaintance, huh?" she said, eyes sparkling. "I have those, too. Very handy for leads. Will I be photographing anything today? I rarely carry this just for exercise." She hefted the camera bag.

"We'll see," I said. "We don't often print pictures because it's costly, but I like to have them for reference. Can you develop them as well?"

"Barely. I plan to get better at it here. I met your developer today and decided I could use some time in that dark room with him." She waggled her eyebrows. I gave her a weak laugh, trying unsuccessfully to remember if someone semi-attractive worked in the darkroom. I gave up and went on.

"I'd like to get over to Panrose Electric as well, to get their side of it. This is just the beginning of my investigation."

"Oh, that's swell. I'm so glad I joined up today. I can't wait to see start-to-finish how you do this reporting lark. When Terry told me about this job, I went back and read all the *Journals* I could find. Your articles were my favorite. I'm just too excited to work for you."

"You're not working for me," I said, blushing. "Mac's your boss. We're just working together, that's all." For now, I added in my mind, thinking of the last five. Obviously, though, Felicity was going to be different. She might be the first assistant to quit after only one day on the job when she saw how boring the beginning of an investigation can be.

She kept up a pretty constant stream of talk all the way to Sero's, politely remembering me from time to time and asking questions about everything from my childhood friends to my favorite coworkers to the best places to "grab a bite" while on the job. My head was spinning by the time we were ushered into Mr. Gaines' office, but somehow, I couldn't keep a silly grin off my face.

Gaines wiped that grin away immediately. "I'm not buying anything," he snapped. "I'm a very busy man." He brought to mind the only slightly less hostile Mr. Vangees, whom I'd interviewed in the Blaster Murders. The two shared an uncannily similar inhospitable air.

"We're not here to sell you something, Mr. Gaines," I said patiently, reaching out to shake his hand. "We're here about the hydroelectric generator. I called you last night, remember?"

He frowned. "You said a reporter would be coming, who I assumed would be your boss."

"Actually, I'm the reporter," I said, accepting the reluctant shake he offered me. "My name is Ginnie Harper, and I've written articles for the *Franklin Journal* for several years now. I'll be conducting the interview. This is my… assistant, Miss Jacks."

His face cleared, but only slightly. Felicity had the wisdom to remain silent. I straightened my vest and sat as he did. Holding the button to program the autophone, I began recording. I'd have to teach Felicity how to handle the autophone later: I really should have taught her on our way here, but I hadn't had the presence of mind to do so.

"I've heard you have some concerns about the generator and its effect on the public's health. Would you be kind enough to tell me about that?"

Gaines cleared his throat. "Yes, of course. When Panrose Electric installed that blasted thing, I knew it was going to be trouble. Morislav has done great things for our city, but some of these new machines are simply dangerous. We've tested the water coming through it, and it's contaminated. Reports of an epidemic amongst the fine citizens of the Hill confirm that the water is not only contaminated, but actually deadly as well! It's a crying shame that Luxity allowed Panrose their way."

"What sorts of tests have you done?" I asked, scribbling short-hand notes.

"Several of the chemical sort that my people would have to explain to you," he said, favoring me with a condescending smile. "I'm sure your schooling wouldn't quite have covered it."

"The schooling of many of our readers should be adequate, though," I answered sweetly. "I try to be as thorough as possible. I'm sure you understand: it's a basic requirement of my profession."

He was trying without success to keep a scowl from taking over his rather jowly features. "Then you can set an appointment with my chemists, Miss Hopper."

"Harper," I smiled. "And thank you. What else leads you

to believe that the sickness on the Hill is connected to the generator?"

"I would think it obvious that the only commonality between all these people getting sick is the water that they drink and bathe in," he answered. "Logic tells me that can't be a coincidence. I saw the plans for the generator before they put it in, and I'll tell you now," he jabbed the table with his forefinger, "Panrose has no consideration for safety for their customers. They're only after the money. Follow the money, I always say."

"Quite so, Mr. Gaines," I said, crossing my legs to continue writing on my knee. "What were their reasons for installing a new generator?"

"What else? Attention! If they can get some press over a new-fangled machine, customers will flock to them for the 'modern experience.'" He snorted. "Those poor new money types on the Hill are just the sort to fall for that kind of thing. Always looking for something new and exciting." He glanced at my notepad and cleared his throat again. "Not that that needs to be printed, of course. I only feel sympathy for their plight now." He shifted in his seat. "They couldn't have known that Panrose was taking advantage of them. I place the blame fully on the company, not the customers." His secretary poked her head in the door, and he waved her away with a frown.

"Naturally, naturally," I murmured. "And what led you to taking these tests on the water?"

"Concerned citizens contacted us," he puffed out his chest and pointed at me emphatically. "We have a reputation for honest dealings, you see. Honesty and integrity: that's Sero's highest priority with our customers."

"And they're not even your customers," I said dryly.

He looked taken aback and then recovered and nodded seriously. "It's our responsibility — all of us as members of this community — to look out for each other. That's all I'm trying to do. All I'm trying to do."

Felicity smiled at him, and he turned slightly pink.

"Mr. Gaines," I said, looking over my notes, "What is your history with the Hill community? Why look out for them?"

"Just as I've said, Miss Hopper, just a community member looking out for others. When I see fellow citizens being taken advantage of, I can't help but do something about it. Right the wrong."

"Can you tell us who contacted you for help?" I asked. "I'd like to follow up with them."

He shook his head slowly. "Sorry, so sorry. They came to me in strictest confidence. Didn't want it to come back on them." He shrugged and rubbed his fingers together.

"And what were they afraid of? What exactly would 'come back on them,' as you say?"

He sighed. "There are things in this world of business that you wouldn't understand. Not your fault at all; not your place, not your place. But these important people on the Hill can't risk going against the grain, you might say."

Holding back a sigh of my own, I said patiently, "The *Franklin* won't print their names, Mr. Gaines. I know how to handle a witness in danger of any kind. I'll use the utmost care."

He gave me a condescending smile and sat back in his chair; he was again rubbing his fingers. "I'm sorry. It wouldn't be right for me to betray their confidence, especially to a newspaperwoman."

I lifted my eyebrows. "I see."

"So loyal of you," Felicity breathed, leaning forward. "And completely understandable."

Gaines looked pleased. "I'm happy to help you in any way I can. There are just some lines I may not cross."

"What about the plans looked unsafe?" I asked.

"Their filtering system was completely inadequate," he answered after a pause, now rubbing his hand on his thigh. "The water source requires extensive purification. Some of the new parts that they use for such machinery will break down easily, leaking contaminants into the overflow. Other issues are quite complicated; I'm sure you understand…"

"And what did you do with this information once you found it?"

"Shared it with the Hill inhabitants, of course. And told the authorities. They were not interested." He shook his head sadly. "Sometimes public servants forget they are indeed servants of the public and not the other way around."

My limit of tolerance was topping out, but I scanned my notes for any further questions to help me later. "In the meantime, while this is being resolved, what would you recommend for the safety of the public? Boiling their water? Filtering it themselves?"

"Boiling it won't rid them of the contaminants. And filtering it probably won't either. The best thing to do is bring the problem to Panrose in a way that is impossible for them to ignore."

"So that they can fix the machinery?"

"So they can shut it down! An entirely new generator will be necessary." He eyed us and then leaned forward earnestly. "And be sure to print that Sero Electric is here for all their needs as a concerned and reliable resource."

I gave him a tight smile and gathered my things, clicking off the autophone with a forceful little thwack.

"You've been ever so helpful," Felicity gushed, wringing his hand. "A real community hero, honest."

Gaines beamed as I hid a gag.

Once we were back on the street, Felicity was beaming, too.

"Are the cases always this easy?" she asked.

I studied her, trying to gauge her words. "No," I said. "Usually people are harder to read."

She nodded. "Makes sense. You'd think a man in his

prominent position would have learned to lie better." Her flaming hair flew as she let out a peal of laughter. "Men can be so smarmy! What a grease can!" She imitated him rubbing his fingers and gave a quite realistic scowl. "*You ignorant reporters don't understand nothin'.*"

I allowed myself a small smile as we walked down the street. "You weren't so honest yourself back there." I didn't realize before I met her that eyes could hold so much gallivanting sparkle.

"Oh honey, you're a working girl. You know how to give them what they want to get them to talk. You just don't do it. Why not?"

I hid a smile as I considered her question. She reminded me of Ward, in that she had read quite a lot about me in a very short amount of time. "I suppose I don't care about telling people what they want to hear."

She shook her vibrant head. "I can't understand how you've made it this far in the newspaper biz. But you really are just the cats. This is great. I think we'll make the perfect team. By the by, you are going to teach me how to work that gizmo, aren't you?"

I handed over the autophone. "This gizmo is called an autophone, and yes, I'd love for you to do the recordings."

"Autophone? That doesn't look a bit like my old auntie's tiny organ."

I gave her a blank look. "Oh! The ones that run with punch cards?" I laughed a little. "I suppose Gene hadn't heard of those when he invented this. Look," I pointed, "that button there is the important one. You hold it down to record the voices that need to be picked up by the 'phone. Then you press this one here to start the interview."

She scratched her ear, eying the autophone. "Why two buttons? Why not just record?"

I shivered involuntarily, remembering. "The purpose of

this is to catch only the voices you want on the recording. It filters out the background."

"Ingenious." She was apparently impressed into silence.

I nodded, trying to keep my mind on the present instead of returning to that fateful night at the hospital that still made my blood run cold and my throat rub hoarse from the screaming nightmares. "Yes, it is," I said.

She was watching me carefully, and I realized I had underestimated Felicity Jacks. She was much too intelligent for secrets.

"Was it his? Your former assistant's?"

I coughed, surprised again. "His invention, yes."

Her eyes widened. "His invention. This is a story I really need to hear someday. Don't worry, not today. I know a wounded person when I see one." She expertly dodged a bicyclist as we crossed the street. "But in the meantime, how about that guy?" She hitched her green purse up on her shoulder and jabbed her thumb behind us. "Where do we go next to disprove his baloney?"

Relieved to ponder the job instead of my startlingly insightful new assistant, I took my paper from my vest pocket and jotted down a couple of notes for the future. I'd need to contact some chemists — from a different company if necessary — and follow up on Gaines' dubious explanation of the generator plans. "I say we head directly to Panrose to learn more about the generator."

"We're certain that it's all perfect nonsense, right?"

I pocketed the notepad with a wry smile. "The tests? Yes. The 'concerned citizen source'? Yes. All his talk about the filtering system and overflow? Likely. But being certain after one interview isn't enough. I can be reasonably sure he's lying without being sure that the generator isn't dangerous. We need more information, especially about the sickness, which I've heard from my source is legitimate, and if it is, we need to investigate the supposed 'logical' correlation. Whether or not this generator is tied to the epidemic, we have a lot to investigate." I paused, thinking. "I'm really quite interested in this story," I admitted.

Felicity actually rubbed her hands together with glee. "Can I do the recording?"

3

It was almost dark that evening before I fulfilled my promise to Diggory and unloaded the bundle of donuts I'd purchased from our favorite baker two streets down. The boy and dog had waited for a couple hours, so I was glad to have a special treat to reward them for their patience. A few minutes into our date, I was grinning: Felicity had accompanied me, and Diggory seemed to be getting more than one treat tonight.

"Holy cats, Miss Felicity," he said more than once. "You really have done everything, haven't ya? Have ya lived all over the city?"

I bit into a donut and peered at the powdered sugar peppering Rufus's nose. I was always dubious about what Diggory fed our four-legged friend, but no one could deny that he was as happy as a dog could be.

"Oh, sonny, you have no idea," Felicity said wickedly, crossing her ankles on the curb and stretching her arms luxuriously high in the air. Sugar flitted down from her donut to land on her fiery head. "You name a boarding house or apartment building, and I've lived there. My parents and I never saw eye-to-eye, so I've been on my own since fifteen."

"I'm 'round fifteen now," Diggory claimed.

"Diggory," I said, "Try again. Miss Jacks can spot a liar three blocks away."

He poked his chin in the air, unabashed. "I'm small for my age, but I'll grow. Mr. Marciano said he was tiny as a bean all growing up an' then BAM!" He slapped his hands together, and Rufus jumped to his feet, barking. "He's no less than six feet and a half now." He stared at me with defiance, and Felicity howled with laughter as I soothed Rufus.

"There, you see?" my assistant gasped. "There's a six and a half foot man inside this little urchin here. Some respect, please."

I shook my head at them, pinching my lips together to hold back a chuckle.

"When's the detective goin' to join us then, Miss Ginnie?" Diggory asked, leaning against a trash can and licking the sugar from his filthy fingers. "He's gettin' to be a stranger with how long it's been."

I checked my watch and yawned. "He's working that mob case on the south end, remember? I don't think he'll be popping by for dessert for a while." I sensed Felicity's burning eye on me and avoided looking at her. "That reminds me: I need to check with Daniels on how that mob story is coming." I eyed Diggory. "You're not hanging out with any of Feltz's people, are you? And no more of Lackwit's old crowd?"

I wasn't the only one avoiding eye contact now.

"Nah, 'course not," Diggory mumbled. "They're trouble. Gotta look out for my sister an' all."

"Diggory," I said, worry creeping up on me. "There's more than just trouble there. You heard about that murder last week, didn't you? You can't trust these people."

He scowled darkly at his toeless shoes. "I told ya I wasn't, didn't I? You're worse than ol' Ward for gettin' on a person's back." He crumpled up an old newspaper and tossed it down the street for Rufus to fetch.

I chose to contemplate the sky and breathe deeply instead of shaking some sense into the little scamp.

"So who's this detective?" Felicity asked, examining her fingernails. "I'm awfully keen to know a real live one. My best friend growing up said she was going steady with one once, but she was all malarky. I never believed a word she said." She quit pretending interest in her nails and latched her blue eyes onto me. "How often does he get into big shootouts? What's his name? Is he tall and dreamy?"

Leaving Diggory to extol Ward's virtues (if not his dreaminess), I wiped my hands on my handkerchief and leaned back, thinking of the afternoon's interview with Panrose's owner.

Felicity and I had arrived during lunch, so we'd waited for him for quite some time. I noticed how much busier their office was than Sero's: the secretary was also their switchboard operator, and she didn't pause even to breathe between calls. Cleanly pressed people hurried around — even during the lunch hour — and the general air was one of orderly tumult. They also possessed one of the new fancy wall mounts that showed moving pictures of the countryside. I thought back to Sero's quiet, traditional building and the untucked shirttails of an employee we'd passed on our way to Gaines' office. The shirttail could indicate the aura of the work environment at Sero or it might not; either way, I put more stock in the contrast of Panrose's intent but cheerful looking employees, as opposed to Sero's sulky ones. I could see how Mr. Gaines may feel threatened by Panrose's modern operation. To gauge the competition between them, I decided I ought to inquire into their financial situations.

Remembering I had an assistant, I asked her to check into it. Felicity was expressing her delight at the chance to do some "homework" when Mr. Panrose returned from lunch, his suit slightly rumpled.

"I'm sorry. I didn't know you were coming, or I'd have taken lunch another time," he said, his forehead wrinkling in consternation.

"My apologies, Mr. Panrose," I said, rising to shake his hand. "I wasn't sure I'd need to talk with you today or not. It's very unprofessional of me, I know. But your secretary was very kind in making us comfortable —" I noticed he gave her a nod at this, "and if you just have a few minutes, I'd love to follow up with you on an interview I just conducted with Mr. Gaines at Sero Electric."

I'd wagered that this would hook him, and I was right. He frowned and jerked his suit coat into submission.

"Please. Come inside. It's loud out here; we'll be more comfortable in my office." He held the door open for us.

"Thank you so much," Felicity smiled as she passed him, and he smiled, too, relaxing just a tad. I gave myself a moment to marvel at her power of charm before sinking into one of the overstuffed chairs in his office. Here indeed was an improvement over Gaines: Panrose kept luxury guest chairs. I immediately liked him better.

"I'll try not to take too much of your time," I said. "Mr. Gaines has made some rather bold claims, and we'd like to get your side of the story."

"I thank you for that, Miss…?"

"Harper."

"Miss Harper. What would you like to know?"

"What makes your hydroelectric generator by the Hill different from the ones that Sero Electric uses?"

Panrose settled back into his chair with a deep breath and studied me, thinking. "Well, Miss Harper, and Miss — I'm sorry, I didn't get your name?"

"Jacks," said Felicity.

"Miss Jacks. The hydroelectric generator is one of

Morislav's best ideas. I believe that in ten years we will use only hydroelectricity to power all the city's generators. It's more efficient, cheaper, and cleaner than the standard generators used before."

"I'm assuming this is why you chose this type as opposed to the standard generator?" I asked quickly.

He nodded. "Quite right. The way it works is this: the flow of the water spins a turbine, which powers the generator. A copper coil, also perfectly safe, spins inside a series of magnets, which creates the electricity and makes the generator work, to put it simply. The other type of generator uses fuel to power the generator by combustion."

"Mr. Gaines claims to have seen the plans for the hydroelectric generator," I said, consulting my notes. "Would that have been possible?"

Panrose rubbed his forehead and sighed. "Possible? Yes. Anything is possible. Ethical? Not necessarily. I never received a request from him to see them. But yes, he may have taken hold of them at some point."

"He also claims that the filtering system is inadequate."

A vein stood out on Panrose's forehead. "Oh, did he?"

"His words were, 'The water source requires much more attention to detail. The new parts that they use for such machinery will break down easily, letting more contaminants into the overflow.'" I studied my shorthand, making sure there was nothing else. "Is this assessment accurate?"

"As accurate as most of what comes out of that pompous…" His face was reddening quickly. "I apologize. No, it's not accurate. His statement is pure bluster. I can give you the plans if you'd like, or, more effectively, have one of my engineers show them to you and explain them. There is no filtering system, as there is no need for a filtering system. There is no source of any contamination: the water simply flows through the machine. I assure you, it is completely safe."

He paused, apparently struggling internally. "Mr. Gaines —

and Sero Electric, consequently — have been trying to put us out of business for years. This is not the first instance of them making false accusations, though it is the most public one." He took another deep breath and frowned at me. "He's trying to ruin us, Miss Harper."

"I get that impression also," I said lightly. "You may be assured that no part of my job is to ruin a company through slander. My goal is to tell exactly what is going on. If you have done nothing untoward, you need fear nothing from me."

He relaxed visibly, and this was the moment I was certain that Gaines' claims were utterly false. But there was more I needed to know.

"Mr. Panrose," I said slowly, twining my hands around my knee and leaning forward, "There are reports of a sickness on the Hill; it's even been called an epidemic. If it's not because of your generator, what could cause it? As a man of science, do you have any ideas?"

He leaned back in his chair and drummed his fingers on the desk, frowning in concentration.

"We'll take any ideas — no matter how odd," Felicity added.

His eyes flitted to her and then back to me. "Testing the water is not a bad idea," he said.

"Gaines claimed his chemists had done so, and it was contaminated," I said, "but he wouldn't say how."

Panrose rubbed his head again. "As I said, testing the water *legitimately* is a good idea. It makes sense that it could be carrying a disease. However, if the disease is unknown, I'm not sure how chemists will know what to look for. The victims should be examined carefully to be sure their symptoms are alike enough to warrant commonality. Then a thorough study of their environment, the common elements of their lifestyles, the people they all have in common, their butcher, their suppliers in general — all should be examined." He paused, looking uncomfortable. "And not to be overly dramatic, you understand, but perhaps the claims of this disease have been fabricated."

"I will look into that as well, though I'll tell you that my first source was quite convincing."

He nodded. Then a thought occurred to him, and his brow contracted. "Miss Harper, I've told you that Gaines has tried to discredit us many times. I will not malign him, but I will urge you to be careful — especially if your story sets him in a... er... unattractive light. I don't have precedent to say that he is dangerous, but..." he faltered. "Perhaps it would be wise to be wary. I hope you understand."

"I do," I said. "I'm a very careful person."

Felicity coughed, and I couldn't help but suspect she was covering a laugh.

"I hope it's not too terribly impudent of me to ask about the state of your financials," I said, smiling apologetically.

"Well, it is," he said, returning my smile, "but I'm happy to tell you we are making a very good profit. We're pleased with our success, especially as a young company, and our stockholders are as well."

"Thank you," I said. "I appreciate your candor — and your words of caution."

"So refreshing to talk to someone who doesn't mind teaching us uneducated reporters," Felicity added innocently. "We had a lovely time."

Panrose smiled and shook our hands. "Thank you for stopping in and getting the entire story. I appreciate your efforts to make this messy situation less... well, messy."

"And thank you for seeing us at such short notice. I apologize for barging in on you. Have a lovely day."

We waved at his secretary as we left, and she gave us a harried grin before jumping back into her work. Panrose stopped to murmur something to her and then saw us to the front door.

"If you have any more questions, don't hesitate to call or stop by," he said.

We voiced our thanks again and left, starting the long walk back to the *Journal* to type up our findings and brainstorm our plan for tomorrow.

———

I jolted back to the present. It was getting dark, and the last sooty trails of the old factories were burning orange in the setting sunlight as the lampposts buzzed to life, creating the glow that gave our city its name. I jumped a little as Felicity said, "So you're seeing this Detective Ward often, are you, Ginnie?"

Diggory jabbed her familiarly in the ribs. "They ain't dating. Miss Harper here'll get all hot in the face if ya say so." He grinned at me cheekily, and I gave him my best scowl.

"You're incorrigible, you know that?"

"It means you're onto something," Felicity whispered to him as he gave her a perplexed look. "Don't worry — I'm a reporter. I'll dig it out of her."

An impending sense of doom struck me — along with a feeling of camaraderie that I hadn't enjoyed with a coworker in quite some time. Recognizing this gave me pause for a moment, and my grin faded. I pushed aside my conflicting feelings and stood, stretching, to tell them goodnight. Felicity and I planned to meet at the *Journal* in the morning before heading to the Hill to give my sister a visit. It was time to investigate this sickness — and to meet my brother-in-law.

4

"Jackson! Tell Mr. Ottison that my sister is here and wants to meet him. And tell Cook that we'll have our tea outside." Chastity looked me over with a critical eye as she led us through her gorgeous home to the back veranda, which was surrounded by trellises of wisteria and roses. "So this is a work visit, is it? Please introduce me to your friend."

"This is Felicity Jacks. Felicity, this is my sister, Chastity Jeff — Ottison."

"Nice to meet you, Chastity Jeff-Ottison," Felicity grinned. Chastity took her hand with a little smile.

"Forgive my sister. I only told her two days ago that I had married. She's not used to my new name yet." She brushed a wisp of hair out of her eyes with a graceful hand and gestured to the table with the other.

"I'm surprised that you're not Harp-Ottison then," Felicity said demurely, turning innocent eyes to me. "I believe there's something you haven't told me, Ginnie Jeff-?"

I gave Chas a look that begged her to relieve me of my new burdensome assistant, and she laughed delightedly. "I say, you're quite the personality, Miss Jacks. Are you new?"

"Everywhere," Felicity said, sitting on the chairs Chas

indicated and smoothing her knee-length skirt. "And every time. I just started at the *Franklin* this week, to be specific. I was lucky to have got your sister. She's the best of the breed over there."

I blushed. "Do you think Edwin will be well enough to meet us?" I asked, sitting gingerly in an ornately carved chair and tracing the designs on the table with my fingertip. "I'd like to meet him, but I wouldn't want to disturb him if he's doing poorly."

Chastity waved away my concern. "Jackson will help him down here if he's woozy. It's time that he met his sister-in-law — and of course, you must see the proof of your story, mustn't you?"

"I could ask you about his symptoms," I said, crossing my ankles. "I'm not a monster."

"Of course not," she said airily. "He'll be fine. Ah, here's the tea."

Tea was becoming a lost art in our city; I'd heard this refrain over and over from my mother as a child, but Chastity was a Jefferson, and Jeffersons would see the art found and propagated as long as they had breath — and in style, too. A maid spread a lace tablecloth over the round table, handing us matching napkins for our laps. I fiddled with mine a bit, unused to this ritual in recent years. Felicity set her purse down with a clunk and watched with dancing eyes as the maid laid the china tea set, complete with gold edging, in the center of the table and handed each of us a cup. Petit-fours, cranberry scones, apple slices sprinkled with sugar, and cucumber sandwiches completed the mid-morning repast. Felicity made herself at home with the Petit-fours while Chastity poured the tea and made believe she saw nothing low-class about my assistant's behavior. I shifted uncomfortably and wished that I'd worn a dress. I'd become so accustomed to my wide-legged trousers since my vow at the construction site during the blaster murders that I hardly thought twice about dressing in the morning. My dresses were pushed into the back corner of my tiny closet and hadn't seen the light of day in months. I could have dusted one off for this occasion, but I'd forgotten entirely about tea time.

Chas had the manners — as always — to decline to comment on my discomfort, and smoothly passed the next few minutes in chit-chat about the *Journal*.

"I hardly read the other papers," she claimed, pouring Felicity a second cup of rose tea. "The *Franklin* is so much more interesting. And of course I can't miss your articles, Ginnie dear. Your writing is much improved since you were ten."

I rolled my eyes and took a sip of tea. "Since you were only eight years old, I don't think your opinion — or memory — counts for much."

"So she's always been writing, has she?" asked Felicity, her eyes sparkling. "What kinds of news did you come up with as a kid?"

"Oh, it was always stories back then, made-up ones, I mean," Chas said, dabbing her lips with a napkin. "Mostly of the fairy-tale type, weren't they? Knights and dragons and maidens and all that. Perhaps a talking wolf thrown in for good measure?" She tapped her chin. "I remember a talking wolf, though I can't recall his name."

"George," I said dryly, memories of Father's scrap paper and a blotchy ink pen filling my mind.

"Oh yes, that's right. He was a regular, if I remember correctly. He and that knight seemed to get in an awful lot of tiffs — regular standoffs, they were. 'An excellent example of foil!'" she mimicked in a childish voice and then sighed long-sufferingly. "You were rather tiresome about your literary terms, dear, even as a child. Our tutors just ate that up about you. Whereas me, they bored me to no end — the tutors and terms, not your stories. Those were entertaining in the best way."

My face was burning, but Felicity was having the time of her life. She'd made her way through several scones heaped with jam, three sandwiches, and most of the Petit-fours. I'd been counting to keep myself pleasant while Chastity rambled so embarrassingly. My last year at home had darkly colored my childhood in my memory, but remembering that cozy attic nook where I'd curled up with a blanket and pen when the muse took me brought back a rush of blissful reminiscences.

"You should write a book," Felicity said; thankfully she had swallowed before speaking. I would have wondered at her reticence had I not been counting how much she was eating. "George and the Dragon."

"I believe that is already a book, dear." Chastity smiled.

Fortunately, Edwin appeared at that moment and spared me the grisly delights of continuing that conversation.

He really did appear pale. Everything about him was pale, including his receding yellow hair, light blue eyes, and faded skin. I wondered if it was his sickness or his natural state. As he moved closer, I noticed odd dark patches on his neck and hands.

"Hello." I stood and smoothed my trousers with a nervous hand. "I'm Ginnie."

"This is my sister," Chastity told him, taking his arm from Jackson, who was supporting him through the door. "She's the one I told you about — the one who works for the newspaper. She's looking into your illness."

He gave me a wan smile. "Nice to meet you." He cleared his throat. It sounded like it hurt him to talk. "I'm sorry that it's not the best of circumstances. I'd like to give my sister a warmer welcome."

"I don't mind at all," I hurried to assure him. "It's been so nice to meet you. Hopefully, I can help."

"Very kind of you," he said, pressing his shaking hand to his stomach. "I'm glad Chastity brought you over."

"This is Ginnie's friend Felicity, Edwin." Chas turned to him. "She works at the paper, too."

"Nice to meet you."

"Will you sit with us?" I asked, pulling out a chair. He looked unsteady on his feet, even with Chastity supporting him. He glanced at Chastity, who nodded.

"For a little time, yes."

"The sandwiches are delightful," Felicity said. She would know, as half of them were gone, thanks to her. She handed him the platter, and he took one, looking queasy. Chastity poured him some tea, which he raised to his thin lips without adding sugar or cream. Watching him out of the corner of my eye, I nibbled a sandwich, conceding to Felicity's opinion. The ratio of cream cheese, dill, and cucumber was superb. Yes, cucumber sandwiches like this made discarding tea time seem a travesty.

Edwin's face was pinched. Was he in constant pain? How horrid for him, I thought, concerned.

"How long have you been ill?" I asked after he'd placed a half-eaten sandwich on his plate.

"Hard to say," he said. "It started slowly. I didn't notice at first, and then I thought it was nothing serious. But after several months, it just got worse and worse."

"So it's been several months?" I was jotting notes in my lap, trying to be inconspicuous about it. Most people feel nervous about having their words recorded. Edwin needed no more frayed nerves.

"At least."

"Over a year," Chastity said. "I remember you complaining during the garden party at your parents' house last summer."

"I suppose you're right," he said faintly. "You'd remember better than I."

"And you hadn't started a new diet? Changed any staff members? Anything like that?"

He looked at Chastity for help. "I haven't the foggiest idea."

Chastity put down her teacup. A sweet-smelling breeze wafted over us; I breathed in the scent of wisteria and let the knot in my stomach loosen.

"We'd only been married a few months, but we kept all the staff members you already had when I came, and Cook would never hear of us touching her recipes." She smiled dourly. "I brought my maid with me, but she wouldn't have introduced anything... harmful to the household."

"And something like this doesn't run in your family?" I was grasping at straws.

He shook his head. "Excellent stock, my dad always said. Healthy as horses." He grimaced.

"Do you know anyone else who's sick? Do they have the same symptoms?"

"Old Fred, next street over, has had an awful season with his stomach," he offered.

"And Benevolence next door," Chastity said. She started ticking names off her fingers. "Luke over on Leaf Street, Sarah, his wife, their daughter Diana, Mrs. Pershing, two houses down, and the entire George Miller household." She frowned, staring at the sky. "There are others, but I can't remember them at the moment."

"And you're sure they have the same symptoms?"

"Ginnie dear, you don't go around asking everyone about their constitution," Chastity said with an arched eyebrow. "But all of them are chronic — it's been months."

I was at a loss, wishing I'd consulted a doctor before coming — or planned more questions. But if Edwin's doctors hadn't concluded anything...

"Your doctors: what have they said? Have they treated others in the area?"

Chastity put down her teacup. "Dr. Mullivan and Dr. Jones treat most of the patients in this area, and I told you what a load of nonsense they concocted. Poor Edwin." She patted his leg, looking concerned.

Edwin was indeed looking very poor. Chastity waved to Jackson, who had apparently been waiting just inside for this very signal. He appeared almost instantly at my brother-in-law's side and helped him up.

"I'm really sorry for all the questions." I couldn't help feeling as though I'd badgered him, though we all knew why I was there.

"Not at all, not at all. It was lovely to meet… you…"

As the door closed on them, Chastity sighed and turned back to me.

"I'm afraid we have been little help." She folded her napkin slowly and placed it beside her plate before looking at me wistfully. "But it has been lovely to have tea again. Much like old times." She smiled, and I was struck by all the years we had lost.

"What was it like…" My throat closed up and I couldn't finish the question.

"What, dear?"

"When I left… You were young, and…"

A shadow passed over her face. It was merely a robin flying low overhead, but for a moment, I imagined a deep pain etched on young, fashionable features.

What had it been like to have her sister, her first playmate, first best friend, *leave* and never return? I remember the last year in my parents' house being a haze of intense work and of darkness, the darkness that descended upon me with Nathaniel's death. I remember nothing of Chastity during that time. She had lost me before I left.

"Life went on," she said lightly. "Mama suffered most, but Papa was too angry to talk about it."

I closed my eyes briefly as my insides shriveled.

"But I understood, Ginnie," she said quietly. "You made your choice. It was not ours to make. I was young, but I understood that much." She met my eyes with twins of my own — hazel light reflecting hazel light — and smiled. "And you're happy, aren't you? In your funny little life with street urchins and deadlines and typewriters? I can see it in your face. You're happy there."

I nodded, holding her gaze. "I am. Truly happy. But I'm sorry for any pain I caused you. I can't make it up to you, and I am sorry."

"You can't make it up to me? My dear girl!" She tossed her head and laughed. "There are a thousand ways to make it up to me, and you've already begun! Tea time is the best peace offering I can imagine."

I smiled and shook my head. "You're obsessed. Just like Mama."

"Rightly so," Felicity piped up, her mouth full of a strawberry tart.

Chastity chuckled and shook her finger at me. "I'll convert you, you renegade. And there's always the matter of the dress and the party."

"Are you ready to go?" I turned hurriedly to Felicity. "We shouldn't infringe on her hospitality anymore, I'm sure."

Chastity laughed and stood. "I'll win this one, dear sister. You're older, but I'm more stubborn. Do watch the step on the way out."

She hugged me, enveloping me in the scent of roses, and I gave her an extra squeeze for good measure.

"Take care," I said, meaning it, as we reached the door. She smiled. "You as well."

"I'll let you know what I find — if I find anything," I said, trying not to get her hopes up.

"The best reporter in Luxity is on the case!" She waved as we walked out to the street. "I know I'll hear all about it soon."

5

That afternoon found my new assistant and I at our desk, heads bowed over my notes, listening to the interviews we'd conducted on the autophone.

"I'll eat this gorgeous new hat if Sero Electric hasn't made up the whole thing," Felicity declared, wiping crumbs off her lap. Chastity had sent several tarts with her; they were all gone, and I hadn't gotten a single one. I tried not to feel too forlorn about this as Felicity continued. "If I hadn't seen your poor brother myself, I'd swear even the sickness was made up!"

Missing my piano-miniature that always clarified my thought process, I tapped a complicated Bach piece on my knee. "Without a doctor checking every sick person on the Hill, we can't be sure the illnesses are related. It really might be a scam, as you're saying. Or a type of flu. Though I wouldn't put it past Mr. Gaines to make it all up," I added under my breath. I'd met plenty of unpleasant people, but he had irked me beyond most.

"If he had the brains, which he doesn't," Felicity said matter-of-factly. "I'd say he sabotaged the generator to make people sick."

I couldn't deny that the thought had occurred to me as well. "It's an interesting theory," I said. "What did you find out about their financial situation, by the by?"

She frowned at her watch. "I'm expecting a morsie any time now. I have a friend at the bank who's checking their accounts."

My fingers paused their tapping. "Is that… legal?"

She shrugged. "He said it would be quick. The bank doesn't get much business in the middle of the week. I expect his answer… ah! Here it is." A thin slip of bright pink paper scrolled out of her morsie. The lines around her mouth were smug as she handed it to me. "Predictable."

<SERO STEADY FOR SEVERAL YEARS STOP GAINES ACCOUNT MIDDLING STOP PANROSE RISING QUICKLY STOP HOPE THAT HELPS STOP>

A pang of conscience struck me, but I added the note to the stack on my desk. "Not exactly a clear-cut motive."

Felicity shook her head. "Panrose is growing! What happens when one company grows and the other stays the same? We built our economy on competition, didn't we? No matter what those lovely socialists would have us do. What about Panrose's claim that his generators will someday power the city? Hmm? Sero is going under if they don't do something soon." She leaned forward, eyes sparkling. "Which they have."

I shook my head, seeing a lesson to be made. "A proper reporter doesn't jump to conclusions. We've got to get more information. I'd like to investigate your idea of sabotage. Will you call Panrose?"

Felicity deflated at my rebuke but perked up again immediately. "Right away, captain!" She saluted. "So I'm asking him if they've checked the generator lately?"

I nodded, ignoring the dramatics. "I'll call Dr. Mullivan and Dr. Jones. Maybe they'll give me something that can tell us if the sickness could have anything to do with water or not.

We really can't ignore Gaines' allegation until we've disproven it."

Felicity paused with one finger poised over our desk phone. "Have you got the preliminary story written for Mac yet? It's going to be so juicy!" She sighed with delight and framed a headline with her other hand. "'Local Business Man Claims Mass Poisoning by New-Fangled Generator!'" She paused, then continued wickedly. "'Ogre disguised as Mr. Gaines of Sero Electric took time away from his normal sabotage routine to lie to our reporters. Mr. Gaines is a bigot and lazy, but residents on the Hill are ready to point the finger with him at Panrose Electric for their efficient new machinery!'"

I gave her a little push, biting back a smile. "Go do your job, Felicity Jacks. Leave the writing to me."

I had to admit to myself that she had talent as I watched her sashaying figure striding over to a quiet corner with the phone to call Panrose. Her exuberant style of "writing" reminded me of Prudence's. Pru had written with unholy relish, exposing the scandals of countless no-goods in her weekly gossip column.

I missed Pru. I remembered the last time I saw her, laid out in a coffin paid for by her colleagues, resplendent in red hair — dyed, unlike Felicity's — and a smart suit. We'd buried her holding peonies, the flowers I'd chosen for my brave best friend. Seeing peonies in flower shops still made my heart ache and my eyes water.

I shook myself. It had only been a couple of days, but I knew I was holding back from a genuine friendship with Felicity. I shuffled the papers on my desk and found a directory in my drawer. As I ran my finger down the alphabetized row, looking for a Dr. Jones, I debated with myself. Should I try to guide her, steer her from the same sensationalism that Pru had been so hungry for, that had eventually led to her demise? I winced. I found Jones' code and tapped it into my morsie. What if Felicity didn't listen to me? Was there any reason to suggest she would?

I finished my message to Jones, then sat back in my chair with a thump. If I'd known that losing my friends would send me spiraling down this hole, perhaps I would never have made them in the first place.

Felicity came bouncing back, radiant with the fun of tasks she'd never done before. "Panrose said they checked the generator yesterday right after we left, and it hasn't been touched. I say, isn't this a lovely mysterious mystery? I can't make heads or tails out of it!"

The smile crept onto my face before I could restrain it. No, I wouldn't forego friendships for fear of losing them. Some people were just too entertaining for such self-preservation.

6

Drs. Jones and Mullivan gave me nothing helpful. Both were reticent about sharing information about their patients, and neither would tell me anything beyond their opinions that there was a mild flu going around, nothing like the 1918 influenza (according to Mullivan) or that each patient had their own unique issues and the situation should certainly not be confused for an epidemic, which was a ludicrous claim (according to Jones). I called my own medical source, a doctor who made home visits to Park residents, but he could only give me a list of ailments that fit their symptoms, all of which I'd heard before, and none of which seemed plausible for this sort of chronic illness.

Felicity wanted to write up a story for Mac right away, but I held back. We had nothing like enough information to start a story. We were no nearer the truth than we were two days ago when Chastity came to me. Stomachs rumbling, we parted ways in the evening, agreeing to meet at the office bright and early.

Unfortunately, it wasn't early enough to avoid Mac's ire.

"HARPER!"

I could hear his bellowing as soon as I walked in the door.

Now what? I thought as I climbed the steps. I found out as soon as I was within shouting distance of his desk.

"What is this?" He threw down a newspaper. It slapped open at my feet, and its contents slithered out. I leaned down and picked it up, my heart thumping in my ears as it always did when he yelled at me. The paper was the *Blue Rose*, the primary newspaper for the Hill residents, and the headline on the front page made my pounding heart sink right down into my shoes.

"'City Scientist Proves Epidemic Started With Panrose'?" Mac growled. "Exactly how did someone else write this story before you?"

I scanned the article, my hands shaking. Gaines had known I would not write the story the way he desired it written, and he had reached out to the *Blue Rose* and a Dr. Sylvester, who had supposedly done a demonstration yesterday (Gaines acted quickly, I thought bitterly) proving that the components of the Panrose hydroelectric generator, when combined with the composition of the water that supplied residents of the Hill, produced a deadly chemical that, if left untreated, could lead to severe illness or even death. Who was this Dr. Sylvester, I wondered, and how had Gaines reeled him in to his cause? Lost in thought, I jumped as Mac roared, "Well? What do you have to say for yourself?"

"I'm sorry that I didn't know about the demonstration," I said, keeping my tone even with an effort. "It looks as though Gaines personally invited the reporter from the *Blue Rose*."

"You've been sitting on information for two days! Why don't I have a story in my newspaper yet?"

"I haven't gotten to the bottom of the story," I said. "There's more going on than the generator, I'm sure of it. When I have the complete story, I'll get it to you, I promise."

"That's not good enough, Harper! The story will be cold and dead like these invalids by then. We've got to keep the presses hot! I want something today." He jabbed his finger into his desk like a hammer hitting an anvil. "*Do — you — understand?*"

I nodded. "I'll do what I can."

"Do better! Now get out!" He picked up a cigar from his desk, where it was ready to light a stack of papers, and jammed it into his mouth. "And tell that assistant of yours to quit flirting with the advertising department boys!"

Closing the door behind me without a word, I didn't notice till I got downstairs that my hands were still shaking. I smoothed my trousers as I strode quickly to my desk, where Felicity sat, painting her nails and scanning the notes from yesterday.

"Good morning," she said brightly. "Writing or interviewing first?"

"Could you hear…?"

"Oh yes. It was loud enough, but I also did a teensy bit of eavesdropping on the stairs. He's full of bark, isn't he? Does he bite?"

"It takes a while for him to bite," I admitted, thinking of how long it took for him to fire Prudence. "He's mostly harmless."

"Oh goody. He'll be fun to stir up, then." She capped her polish and blew on her nails. "So what will it be?"

I took a moment to reorganize the desk while I decided how to answer. "I'm going to jot off a quick story just in case, and then we'll call Panrose. No, scratch that. I'll write and you call Panrose. See what their response is. Take notes." I reached out to give her a pad of paper, but she was already across the room with the phone. I sighed and squared my shoulders, pulling the cover off my typewriter.

Half an hour later, I had a small rough draft of a piece that outlined our progress in the investigation with no conjecture or fear-mongering. Felicity was still on the phone, one arm crossed under her chest, leaning against the wall and laughing. Two of the reporters closest to her were shooting her furtive looks. I rolled my eyes and waved to her to let her know I was done. She gave me a nod, laughed one more tinkling laugh, and hung up, making her way back to me.

"You were on with Panrose the whole time?" I raised my eyebrows, checking my watch.

"No, silly. That was my friend, Will, who works with the fellow who reported on the demonstration yesterday for the *Blue Rose*. They gave me the whole run-down. The reporter said that a Dr. Sylvester mixed water from one container and a shard of metal from another container, supposedly from the generator, and it made a nice puff of smoke and turned a lovely grey color for just a second. Then he fed it to a mouse, which died in a jiffy." She snapped her fingers. "Must have been very engrossing, but that poor mouse! I'd like to give this Dr. Sylvester a good kick in the pants."

"I… What did Panrose say?"

"Panrose? Oh yes. He was pretty mad — well, furious, really. He said the demonstration was a load of hogwash and that Gaines must have bribed Dr. Sylvester. I quote: 'Only a complete fraud would pull a trick like that simply for press coverage.' End quote." She grinned. "He's going to do his own demonstration later this morning and wants us there post-haste."

"But is Dr. Sylvester a fraud?" I asked, rising and tucking the autophone in my pocket. "Who is he? We need to —"

"Oh, I did." She waved airily. "He's a professor at the university. A chemist. The *Blue Rose* fellow said you can tell he's a scientist — the bookish type." She wrinkled her nose. "Sickly looking. You know what I mean. He looks to be head of the department before too long but doesn't get out into society much. His health, I think. No family. Pretty well off, though, it looks like. He drives a Rolls, and his briefcase was fine leather." She stroked her gloves dreamily. "Will — that's my friend at the *Blue Rose* — worked at the glove factory with me. He's a terrific dancer."

I shook my head at her in disbelief. "Did you learn anything else?"

She pouted her lips and stared at the ceiling, tapping her pen on her chin. "Nope. Nothing relevant to the story, at least. But Will told me the funniest story about the mayor's wife — wait 'til you hear it." She leaned in for the kill, but I cut her off.

"That's all right. I'm not a gossip columnist. Let's go." I started for the door.

Her face fell, and she grabbed her purse before catching up to me, her bright red heels clacking on the floor. "I'm sorry I didn't get more." She sighed. "You write really fast, you know. I didn't have much time to investigate."

An incredulous laugh sprang out of me as I opened the door and waved her ahead. "Felicity Jacks, I think you were born to be a reporter."

Panrose looked like he'd cooled down only slightly by the time we arrived. He ushered us into a large room and seated us with a few other journalists and then hurried out again.

"Hi, Will," Felicity trilled, giving a young, dark-haired man a coy wave. He jumped up eagerly and tripped over another *reporter* on his way over to us.

"Thanks for the invite, Fil," he said, shaking her hand reverently. "I'm awful lucky I got this gig. The guy who went to that presentation yesterday got called out on a different story, so I got to take his place! My luck! Hi," he said, turning to me and grinning. "You with the *Franklin*, too?"

Felicity *tsk*'ed him with a little swipe to his bicep. "This is Ginnie Harper, William! My mentor and boss." She winked at me. "Show a little respect, Mr. New Hire."

Will bowed to me in mock deference. "My sincerest apologies, Miss Harper. I had no idea."

I rolled my eyes. "I can see how you two got along at the factory. How long were you there?"

He scratched his head. "I lost count. Long enough to take her to dinner a few times before she ran off." His smile was endearingly lopsided, much like his hat.

"They kicked him out for drinking on the job," Felicity stage-whispered.

"Hypocrites, the lot of them," he said, shaking his head. "It's great to meet you, Miss Harper. I read all your pieces. Several of the boys at the *Rose* do, too, but don't tell them I told you. They're a bunch of pirates; they all copy you. That murder series you covered last year — everyone still talks about it. I even read it — and that was *before* I got into the newspaper business." He gave me a respectful thumbs-up just as Panrose reentered the room, ushering in a man with white hair strictly parted down the middle and carrying a battered briefcase.

"Sit, sit," Panrose said brusquely. We all sat, Will unceremoniously stealing the seat next to Felicity from a young reporter, who glowered darkly at him. "This is Dr. Lloyd from the university. He is an engineering professor and will prove the absolute safety of the Panrose hydroelectric generator. This," he pointed to a large machine on the table in front of us, "is a working miniature of the generator that we used for demonstrations before the Oak Hill model was built. It is made from the same materials and has the same components, in smaller form. Mr. Barron, if you wouldn't mind…"

A tall man in a finely tailored suit stood and held out a jar that contained clear liquid.

"This is water taken directly from the Oak Hill water supply before it reaches the generator?" asked Panrose.

"Yes," the man said shortly.

"You are Mr. Barron of Oak Hill, correct? No ties to this company whatsoever?"

"Correct."

I was scribbling notes, and Will was patting his vest, presumably searching for paper and a pencil. Felicity was leaning forward on her knees, her camera hanging from her neck. She appeared utterly enraptured.

"I approached Mr. Barron and asked him to do this minor task for us so that we would be above reproach. We had never met before this morning when I chose his house randomly to make my request."

No wonder Mr. Barron looked grumpy. Panrose must have been at his house before the man had even gotten breakfast.

"Dr. Lloyd will now test the water to prove once and for all that the Panrose hydroelectric generator is harmless, perfectly safe, and completely fit to continue providing the best electric service to the residents of Oak Hill." He stepped back and mopped his forehead with a white and gold handkerchief.

Dr. Lloyd took the water from Mr. Barron and silently poured a small amount of it into a machine that he had unpacked while Panrose was speaking.

"This spectrometer," he said in a gravelly voice that caught me by surprise, "tells us about the molecules of the water sample. It will print a chart presently..." (a roll of white paper slid out of one end), "that informs us of the size and amount of the different components in the water. It cannot tell us of any compounds present, but it can tell us if the generator has any effect on the water." He examined the paper and lifted it to show us. He then pulled a different paper from his briefcase and held the two side by side. "This is a chart of the water taken from my home in the Park. You can see that they are almost exactly the same. I can vouch personally for the water in my neighborhood." He paused. "I will now run the water through the generator and test it again. If it is identical to the chart of the Hill water before going through the generator, that is sufficient proof that the generator does not affect the drinking water of Oak Hill."

I glanced at Felicity to see if she had followed this little speech. She was snapping pictures with her camera and looked delighted. Will, on the other hand, scratched his head and peered at the notes of the reporter next to him.

I looked back in time to see Dr. Lloyd take the jar and pour the remaining water into a sort of slide that led to the generator, which hummed to life as the water entered its belly. The water churned out on the other side, and a globe light, powered by the little generator, shone a cheery glow over us as the chemist retrieved the water in a large beaker and introduced it to the spectrometer once more. I jotted a couple of notes about the steady glow of the electric light the generator produced while we waited for the chart that printed moments later. Dr. Lloyd held it up alongside the Hill water chart, and Felicity turned to me with a triumphant smile. Panrose exhaled in relief. The two charts from the Hill were identical.

"As you can see," Dr. Lloyd said, "this generator has not poisoned or otherwise contaminated this water sample. If I may be so bold as to insert my professional opinion, residents of the Hill need not fear Panrose Electric technology for their water supply."

Some Panrose employees standing by Mr. Panrose broke into spontaneous applause. Letting her camera fall and bounce against her chest, Felicity joined them enthusiastically, as did Will, a moment later.

"Dr. Lloyd," I called, my pen poised, "thank you for the demonstration. Could you give us your credentials so we may legitimize this experiment for the public?"

"I taught at the University for thirty-five years," he replied in a rumbly voice, packing his equipment. "My associates can speak for my… legitimacy, as you say."

"And what would you say of Dr. Sylvester, who teaches there?" Felicity piped up.

Dr. Lloyd glowered. "Dr. Sylvester teaches in a different department. I have nothing to say about him. Good day."

"Dr. Lloyd, Dr. Lloyd!" shouted another reporter I didn't recognize. "Your Park water chart isn't the same as the Hill water! What does this mean? Is Luxity's water of unequal quality? Could the Park residents be taking the finest for themselves? What —"

Without further ado, despite the mounting questions, Lloyd jammed a hat on his head, shrugged on his coat, and left the room, hauling his equipment with him.

"It's just too infuriating," Felicity breathed, as we poured out of the building with the rest of the excited reporters. Contrary to her words, she looked happier than I'd ever seen her. "Without Gaines here, we can't see his face when he hears what just happened. What will he do now?" She skipped down the street.

I furrowed my brow and wondered, too. This investigation seemed to be going nowhere. Our suspicions about Gaines were confirmed, but what had we learned? Nothing newer than what we'd guessed already. We still had no idea why the Hill residents were sick — or why Gaines was so intent on damaging Panrose's reputation.

As Felicity and Will yammered on about corruption in the electric companies and setting Dr. Sylvester's reputation on fire, I racked my brain for how to proceed. Ruining Gaines was not on my agenda. I wanted to know why there was an epidemic in Chastity's neighborhood. Perhaps Dr. Lloyd would explain the chart and tell me what different components were in the water; could the slight variance between Hill water and Park water be the key? It didn't sound as though the spectrometer could yield the information I needed, just the individual molecules. Maybe Chastity could introduce me to her ill friends? Judging by her response at tea, I mustn't rely on her for that. I surmised she was likely correct about people in her neighborhood not being comfortable talking about their maladies. I stared at the hem of Felicity's bright blue skirt, swishing around her knees in front of me. Perhaps Gaines was the route to follow; perhaps his insistence on framing Panrose was covering up for something else. I just had no idea what that would be.

I realized I had absentmindedly followed Felicity and Will into a cafe that I was nominally positive hosted a speakeasy in the evenings. It was popular at the moment, and the noise jolted me out of my reverie.

"What do you want to eat?" Felicity yelled to me over the clatter of plates and noisy patrons. I spotted Will's slim form squeezing through the masses to the counter. "Will's treat!"

I hesitated, and a wave of newcomers carried her forward. "Never mind! I'll order for you!"

Feeling near suffocation, I extricated myself from the crowd and escaped back out into the late morning light of Luxity, where I promptly breathed in the fumes of a ripe garbage can next to me. I covered my mouth, coughing, and my morsie dinged. Dabbing my watering eyes and removing myself from the vicinity of the stench, I read the slip of paper.

<CASE OVER STOP ARE YOU CERTAIN DANIELS WILL WRITE IT PROPERLY STOP WHAT ARE CHANCES OF YOU WRITING IT INSTEAD STOP HOW ABOUT LUNCH STOP>

I shook my head with a small grin. Daniels had been assigned to Ward's mob story when Mac put me on an arson investigation instead. Ward hadn't been happy about it, especially after he met the lackadaisical Daniels, but since we didn't know when Ward's case would wrap up, and since Daniels was new, Mac didn't want me to turn down any more complicated cases for its sake in the meantime. He had Daniels on quick turnaround stories so he'd be available whenever the mob case was finished and needed to go to press the next day. Apparently, that was now.

<AT FRANKS STOP DID YOU GIVE DANIELS AN

INTERVIEW YET STOP> I typed back. It was a good thing I wasn't covering his story, what with Mac wanting a decent article on this electric mess by the evening.

<SEE YOU SOON STOP OF A SORT STOP UNSATISFACTORY STOP>

The corner of my mouth turned up. I had witnessed none of Daniels's interviews, but I could imagine how they would go. Although I hoped he wouldn't turn out to be the type that paraphrased his interviewees' words and then put the paraphrase in direct quotes, I thought I might be wishing for too much. Felicity and Will came chattering out of the cafe, their hands full of food, just as I stowed my morsie.

"The city's best frank for you, Miss Harper." Will bowed as he handed me the hot dog wrapped in greasy paper.

"Thanks," I said. I pulled out my thin purse, but he looked shocked.

"You would deny me the pleasure of saying I treated the famous Ginnie Harper to lunch? All the fellows will be jealous. Put that thing away!"

I stowed my purse with a snort of a laugh and took a bite of the frankfurter. It was certainly the best in town, but that wasn't saying much. Will was busily devouring his own, which was smothered in catsup while Felicity munched away on a doughy pretzel the size of her head.

"So what's next?" she managed to say with a full mouth.

I hesitated. I wasn't sure I wanted to introduce my assistant to my detective friend yet, but since he was already on the way, it was probably too late.

"What kind of story are you going to write?" I asked Will. It was odd speaking to a reporter from another newspaper; we would be considered competitors even though the *Blue Rose* and the *Franklin Journal* usually covered different types of stories. In this case, the overlap had brought us together, and I was interested to see what he would do. I was also intrigued because Will had said that his coworkers used my stories, and though I admitted it was lazy of them, I was encouraged that my findings were being spread farther than the *Franklin*'s reach.

Will wiped catsup from his chin with a pocket handkerchief and grinned unapologetically. "Oh, we're doing a full page spread on this one. The drama is too good to miss, and the whole thing is about *our* readers, remember. Everyone on the Hill reads the *Blue Rose*. They'll want the full juicy story."

"Don't you think they want the actual story, though?" I asked resignedly. It was silly that I bothered; I'd had this conversation a thousand times with different coworkers. "Rather than focusing on the drama, isn't it important to tell them the truth behind why they're sick and why Mr. Gaines is determined to frame Panrose?"

Will waved away my concern for his readers. "All of that will come up eventually. In the meantime, we'll be selling papers faster than we can print them, and *my* name will be on the front page." A dreamy expression took over his boyish face. "I'll dig up everything I can that's suspicious about Dr. Sylvester for tomorrow's article. This afternoon I'm writing about the demonstration and then I'll do a full article on Dr. Lloyd."

Felicity met my eyes pleadingly. "We're writing something about the demonstration, aren't we?"

I sighed. "Yes."

"People *do* need to know what a scumbag that Gaines is, don't they?" She sounded like she was trying to reason with a toddler.

"All we're going to give them is the facts," I said. "Leave the embellishments to the *Blue Rose*." I winced. "No offense, Will."

"Embellishment is our goal," he shrugged, looking unhurt. "Can't cater to the rich without a bit of sensationalism."

"Can't cater to *anyone* without sensationalism," Felicity

muttered. Then she brightened. "I know. Let's get a statement from the university head on both professors. Or, I know," she snapped her fingers, "Let's get a quote from Dr. Sylvester. *Exclusive* to the *Franklin*." She scowled with mock ferocity at Will, who backed off with his hands raised good-naturedly.

"I know when I'm not welcome anymore. I'll leave you ladies to it. Very nice meeting you, Miss Harper. Bye, Felicity." He tipped his hat and jogged across the street. "You're welcome for the grub!" he yelled over his shoulder.

"Yes, thanks very much!" I called back.

Felicity cocked her head as she studied my face.

"He liked you," she said. "And don't worry. He knows he does his work differently than you." She shrugged. "He's fine with that. He told me the guys over at the Rose really do like your stuff, even without embellishments." She paused and then gave me a side smile. "He says they read the Harper news to find out what's really going on."

My face heated with both pleasure and embarrassment. "Felicity…"

"Yes?"

"I think now might be a good time to tell you my operating rules."

She scrunched her face together and pursed her lips. "That sounds absolutely riveting — oh wait, no. Dead boring." She grinned. "OK, I'll listen. Shoot."

"Just four rules. The first is to act independently."

"No assistants?" she widened her eyes at me in mock consternation.

"No — no bribes. No money under the table. I can't get so close to a source that I'm not willing to report their wrongdoing."

"And the others?"

"I try my best to be accountable and transparent. Honest. And I always strive to minimize harm." My gaze followed Will's disappearing form. "I've seen a lot of trouble come from sensationalism. I must protect my sources, especially if they've given me information that could get them in trouble. This is… very important to me."

She nodded earnestly. I hadn't expected a captive audience for my brief lecture, but I pressed my advantage while I had it.

"The last one is the one you already know. I'm always going to seek the truth and report it, no matter what it is." My thoughts turned to Nathaniel and then to Gene. "Truly, no matter what it is."

When I looked at Felicity, I was afraid that those blue eyes were penetrating into my memories. She opened her mouth; my stomach clamped in anxiety over what she was about to ask — and then she saw something over my shoulder, and in a split second, the look in her eyes turned mischievous.

"Ooh, get a slant at that tall guy over there — he's looking right at you. Why, he's coming over here this minute! What a thrill!"

It was Ward. I felt myself relax instantly. Throwing the hot dog paper in the trash, I waved, wiping my hands on my trousers absentmindedly. He gestured to the trash.

"I see you ate already."

"There are more inside," I offered. "And fewer customers now to wrangle. It was a madhouse half an hour ago. Best frankfurters in the city."

He raised his eyebrows. "That's not saying much."

I grinned. "How did it go?"

"Trial's in two months," he said, knowing what I meant. "It's in the prosecutor's hands now. He thinks there's more than enough evidence to convict."

"That's great news," I said, watching him with narrowed eyes. "So what's wrong?"

"It should have been harder to catch him." His eyes were shuttered. I could tell he hadn't truly come off the job yet. "I can't help but think someone behind the scenes was pulling strings we didn't see."

"You always say most of these guys are pretty dim. You don't think it was just a lack of cleverness?"

"No… not this time." He came back to the present and studied Felicity. "Who's your friend?"

"Felicity Jacks," she said, obviously thrilled to be noticed. "You're much too tall for me, but just right for Ginnie. You must be the detective friend. Ward?"

He shook her hand, baffled but amused. "Quite right. She talks about me, does she?" He gave me a side eye, and I blushed, furious, as Felicity continued glibly.

"Oh no, not yet, but Diggory does. He's a little more clear-sighted. Great kid. So what kind of action did you see? Have you been shot? Any mobbers try to kill you? It must be terribly exciting."

"Not too much, yes, no, and sometimes it's very boring, actually. Very nice to meet you, Miss Jacks. It's about time Miss Harper got another assistant."

"I had one two weeks ago," I said in annoyance.

"One that will stick around," he said. "I'm going to get a frank."

"I like him," Felicity announced as he disappeared inside.

"I'm so glad," I said dryly.

"Yes." She ignored me and tapped her chin with a bright blue fingernail. "I think he'll do just fine. Well caught."

"I don't have any idea what you're talking about," I said, taking out my notepad and pencil. "But I do think we should figure out what to do next with our story."

Ward appeared a moment later, hot dog in hand, as Felicity and I sat on a bench, debating our next move.

"Is this why you won't write my mob case?" he asked, standing beside me and taking a large bite of his frankfurter.

"Partly, yes. Daniels will do fine, Ward, really. I'm not so sure about us, though." I raked my hand through my hair in frustration.

"It's a killer story," Felicity said, eyes dancing. "All these rich people dying on the Hill and two companies fighting it out with science experiments and bribes. You couldn't make it up if you tried."

Ward raised his eyebrows. "What's this about people dying?"

I rubbed my head. "There are a lot of people sick on the Hill right now — chronically sick. My brother-in-law is one of them."

He turned to me in surprise. "Reconnecting with family, are you?"

I traced a ridge on my trousers with my finger. "My sister, Chastity, came to find me a few days ago. She said her husband was sick, and she wanted me to find out why. It's led us to a rather interesting mystery."

His face darkened. "I see. She couldn't look you up earlier, of course."

Felicity quirked an eyebrow at him, and I saw a flash of understanding pass between them.

"It's not like that," I protested. "I gave you the short version. But anyway, Edwin has been ill for over a year, and Chastity said there are several others who are sick, too. Gaines of Sero Electric claims it's the hydroelectric generator that Panrose Electric put in for the Hill residents. He says it's polluting the drinking water, and he had a scientist do some sort of fraudulent experiment to prove it. Then Panrose had another scientist disprove it, and now here we are, and I don't know where to go next." I paused. "And meanwhile, people *could* be dying."

Felicity looked more sober than I'd ever seen her, and Ward drew his brows together in thought. "The hydroelectric generator? Sero must be desperate. There's clearly no basis for health suspicions with that machine. It's flawless."

Felicity looked curious, like she was about to interrupt, so I said, "He reads *The Current*. Keeps up on all the latest electrical gadgetry." She appeared suitably impressed.

"What sort of illness is it?" Ward asked, still focused on his train of thought.

I gestured helplessly. "That's part of the problem. The doctors don't agree on what it could be, but Chastity said it's stomach pain, vomiting, muscle pain…"

"Edwin could barely talk without clearing his throat," Felicity added.

"He's terribly thin," I said. "And his skin doesn't look healthy. One doctor says it's influenza, another thought it was ulcers… Chastity doesn't believe either of them."

Ward was thinking hard with his eyes shuttered again. "This sounds familiar… oddly familiar," he said. "The suspicious claims, the water, the symptoms of the illness…"

I sat up straighter. "Truly? And it wasn't just the flu?"

"No," he said slowly, "The flu doesn't last that long. Let me think a moment."

We waited, me tapping a melody on my thigh, Felicity practically wringing her hands in excitement. A Rolls Royce cruised by us, clearly lost. I thought about jogging over to give them directions, but they moved on before I could decide.

Then Ward's eyes darkened with remembrance. "Yes, that's it: I was on a case several years ago where a young boy died. There was an illness in a neighborhood. People thought it was influenza, but the boy's mother and father thought the source was the water. The father was a medic in the war and didn't believe the doctors' diagnoses. When the police decided there wasn't enough evidence and dropped the case, the parents pursued it alone. They were obsessed with their son's death. They stayed in touch with me, let me know how it was going. Then suddenly I quit hearing from them." He paused.

"And that was all?" I asked. When he nodded, I gripped

my pen tightly. "Will you give me their contact information? When exactly was this?"

"Five years ago," he said. He drew a small book from his suit coat pocket and rifled through it. "Here."

I copied down the number he was showing me.

"It gave me the same fishy feeling that I'm getting from your story. I don't know if it'll help at all, but it's possible that they could provide another angle." He put the book back in his pocket with a furrowed brow. "Would you let me know what happened to them when you find out?"

Tense, I looked at Ward and saw the Hunt reflected in his eyes, too.

"You're not saying you think there could be a connection, are you?" I asked slowly.

He didn't answer me.

"What fun!" Felicity said, startling us by clapping her hands and bouncing on the balls of her feet. "Though it's probably just a coincidence."

I knew what Ward was going to say before he said it.

"As a rule, Miss Jacks, I don't believe in coincidence."

7

The afternoon kept us in a flurry of activity. I finished my story for Mac, allowing Felicity to add a couple of paragraphs, which I edited carefully. She was so giddy over being printed that she fluttered around like a ninny for at least a quarter of an hour before I could corral her into doing our next assignment. First, I sent Ward's lead a message asking for an interview. I received a positive reply as I was writing out a list of suppliers to the Hill. Mrs. Jacobs and I set a time for that evening to meet, and then I pulled Felicity out the door. I was determined to discover for certain if there were any contaminants in the water that could make someone sick. We spent the rest of the afternoon around the Hill, where we collected water samples from five residents' houses, including Chastity's. As readers of the *Blue Rose*, the residents we approached not only consented to give us some of their water but also detained us to gossip about Gaines' demonstration, fishing for more information on the generator. Before I could stop her, Felicity declared to one such housewife, "Catch the news tomorrow and you won't be disappointed! But get the *Franklin*," she said wickedly. "The *Blue Rose* goes in for too much sensationalism. You want to subscribe to the *Franklin* for the real news."

The woman's eyes gleamed with a curiosity that I recognized instantly. Judging by her conversational prowess as a gossip, I estimated that she'd have successfully spread Felicity's words to the entire Hill within the next two hours.

I hauled my impish assistant away with a sort of despairing admiration.

"She'll have that all over the neighborhood within a couple of hours," Felicity protested with satisfaction as I gave her a shake of my head.

"I agree completely. And that's not our job."

She put her nose in the air. "I believe in taking opportunities as I see them, Miss Harper." Her eyes widened innocently. "Would Mac expect any less?"

I groaned and let a laugh escape before I noticed it sneaking up on me. "Felicity Jacks…"

"Yes?" The mischievous look was back on her freckly face.

I turned south to leave the Hill and heaved a gusty sigh. "If you and I don't pan out, I will be sure to put in a good word for you with the sales department."

She gave me a cheeky grin and fell into stride beside me, keeping up effortlessly in her completely non-sensible shoes.

After being sure the water samples were secure in their covered jars, we stopped to chat with several suppliers to the Hill: the butcher on South Seed Street, the bakery next door, the fresh market down the road, and the cannery two streets over. None of them had changed their ingredients or the way they did things in the last two years. Their products were consistent, their suppliers were consistent, and there was no reason to suspect they'd have a grudge against their customers. They were long-established businesses, catering to the well-off folk on the Hill for the last ten years.

"We don't have to change things," the affluent butcher told me as he cut steaks with blood-spattering speed. "These nouveau riche just want to know that they are getting the type of quality that the long-standing Park residents get." He abandoned his great knife with a loud thunk on the red-streaked counter and wiped his hands on his spotted apron. "They'll change almost anything else with the fashions, but when it comes to meat, they want the same cut of prime rib that old Baughmann gets for dinner every Friday night." He slid a large, slimy haunch to the center and picked up his knife again. "Meat is meat." Loud thwacks accented the slap of the door as it closed behind us.

I was both disappointed and excited. We'd checked another task off my list, and though we hadn't found the cause of the illness yet, we had eliminated several more possibilities. If I'd thought that Felicity would wear down after a long afternoon asking the same questions of multiple people and businesses, I was wrong. She was as chipper as ever, and I found to my surprise that her energy actually increased mine. We practically jogged to the university to find a Professor Laining, who had agreed to test our water samples for us.

"It's no trouble at all," she assured us, taking the samples with gloved hands and giving us a jolly smile. "Would you like to sit down for a moment? You're flushed like you've just been running!"

"Thanks," Felicity said, plunking down on the wooden chairs crammed in the space between the professor's desk and the wall. "You know, I assumed you'd be a man; I was awfully surprised to find you in a skirt."

Professor Laining's eyes twinkled. "I've gotten to where I enjoy surprising people," she said. "It's nice to see a couple of young women here as well. We're both in male careers, aren't we? I feel positively macho by the end of the day here, surrounded as I am."

Felicity laughed. "I haven't got nearly as much time as I'd like with the boys at the *Franklin*." She shot me a coy look.

"Miss Harper here keeps me running around town all day. But I can't say I complain. There's never a dull moment."

"I know what you mean," she murmured, inspecting the jars. "Of course, I get my excitement from beakers and chemicals. But you never know when you might blow something up." She rustled around her tidy desk for a moment. I sank into the chair next to Felicity, watching the professor in unashamed fascination. "In fact, just the other day I combined two chemicals that I never have before (I was thinking of something else and wasn't paying attention), and would you know it, they exploded? My classroom still smells like burnt toast. It makes me smile every time I go in for class." She squinted at her shelf and pulled down an instrument that was making an odd thrumming noise. "Dr. Sylvester used to say he never knew when he'd come in to find me disintegrated on the floor."

Felicity gave me a knowing glance.

"These professor types can be awfully stuffy," she said, swinging her legs so that her shoes almost flipped off her feet. "Dr. Sylvester sounds like quite a yawn."

"A bit, yes. But I monitor him. You want to be in his good graces if you want to go anywhere in this city."

"I thought he didn't get out much," Felicity said carelessly. "Looks like the indoor type."

"Oh certainly. But he knows people. And I've got an uphill climb as it is — most people look askance at a woman with so much education beneath her belt." She smiled, adjusting rimless spectacles. I wondered if people looked askance at her for other character traits as well.

"Don't you get bored sometimes?" Felicity asked, glancing around the tiny office.

"Oh, sometimes I do — or the students give me lip — but then I just imagine what I'd use to poison them, and it gives me a nice little diversion until I can smile and move on."

Felicity laughed out loud, and I studied the professor with

a mixture of respectful fear and professional interest. There was no telling when I might investigate her in the future. She was just the type to make a story interesting very quickly.

She interrupted my reverie by shooing us out. "It's been lovely, but I need some peace to work. I'll send you the results as soon as I am finished. Expect a couple days and don't pester me, whatever you do."

No fear of that, I thought as Felicity dragged me out, eager to meet with the chemistry and engineering department heads. She had coaxed the promise of an interview out of both of them for information on the warring Drs. Lloyd and Sylvester.

I split from her at that point to go back to the *Journal* and prepare for my interview with the Jacobses.

Here I pause. My new wave light sparkles cheerily to my right side, illuminating my tea-stained paper as I write. The light is a present from Ward, dear man, who found out about my evening reminiscences and insisted on a better light than candles for his frugal friend. It was a pretty present and a comfort to have this friendly little flicker that I can turn on and off with a simple hand motion.

This marks the place in my story where everything shifts. I hardly know how to go on. I do this exercise on paper to study my experiences, learn from them, improve as a writer, and dare I say, as a person. If I can understand what I have done and experienced, then perhaps I can become a better version of myself.

So, where do I begin now? Everything leading up to this point is in a way expositional for all that came afterwards.

I am glad that I had Ward by my side when I had no idea what we would soon learn. And yes, Felicity as well, dear Felicity.

Perhaps that is where this second stage began: with the news that Felicity brought back from the university.

———

"I have them!" she cried triumphantly, clutching her purse and waving at me across the crowded, noisy office. "Exclusive quotes from the university heads and, more thrillingly, from Dr. Sylvester, who damns Panrose and Dr. Lloyd with every word. It's too dramatic."

"Well, hand them over," I said tolerantly, extending my palm. "I'll see if we can fit them in."

"Fit them in?" She put her hand over her chest with the gesture of a seasoned actress playing a heartbroken Juliet. "My dear Ginnie Harper, these quotes will make our story! Our readers will be up in arms! Demand immediate action! Throng the streets to—"

"Felicity," I said patiently, my hand still extended. "If you don't hush and give them to me, I'll have you thrown out."

"I can't," she said, scraping her chair over to plop down happily next to me. "They're in here." She tapped her cranium with a blue nail. "Ready? I'll dictate."

"You didn't take notes."

"Why would I?" She looked genuinely curious. "Ok, here I go. Dr. Sylvester said…"

She rattled off his words in a bright voice, giving inflection where I doubted he would have even thought to do so, but I could tell the words were his — there was no hint of paraphrase in the terminology. I typed as quickly as I could, asking her to repeat here and there, and when she'd given me everything from all three men, I removed the paper and stared at it.

"How did you do that?"

"What?" She was applying lipstick in bold strokes, staring into a pocket mirror.

"How did you remember what they said?"

"Oh." She laughed and snapped the mirror shut, smacking her lips together. "I forget. That's why you take notes, isn't it? You don't remember?"

"Yes," I said, raising my eyebrows in disbelief. "That's why everyone takes notes or uses an autophone. No one remembers —" I consulted the paper again, "an entire page of quotes. No one."

She shrugged, tracing her lips with a finger and wiping the excess stain on her handkerchief. "I do. Always have."

When I gazed at her stupidly, she smiled. "It's never been useful until coming here. There wasn't much need for memorizing people's words at the laundry." She giggled as I shook my head at her. "And people don't like it when you quote them back to themselves in an argument. So." She shrugged again. "At least here it's handy as anything — and I don't have to remember to carry a pen."

"Right," I said. When would I stop being flummoxed by my extraordinary new assistant? Could one live in a constant state of befuddlement?

Felicity interrupted my bewilderment. "I found out something interesting," she said. She was staring at me, her usual playful twinkle gone. "The head of the engineering department is related to Morislav somehow or another, and when we talked about this case, he mentioned offhand that Panrose's sole investor is Edward Baughmann. You know, Morislav's partner, the guy who owns Baughmann Industries." Her blue eyes flickered as the information registered on my face.

Gene's father. It was a shock, as hearing that name still was, but it made sense. Morislav's hydroelectric generator, a revolutionary power company leaving behind old ways — yes, that was exactly where Baughmann would see potential.

"Did you say sole investor?" I asked.

She nodded.

"And Sero?" I said. "What about them?"

"I sent a morsie to a friend on my way back," she said, confirming my faith in her. "Sero has multiple investors. The company went public several years ago, and the stock stays pretty steady." She studied me, clacking her fingernail on the seat of her chair. "Baughmann. Jim, in the copy department, said that was your former assistant's name."

I nodded. "You know, we haven't looked into the company's investors. Maybe you should follow up on that."

She relaxed her shoulders, accepting my change of subject. "Are you ready for the interview? Do you think that's going to be it?" She leaned back in her chair and kicked off her shoes. "If I had a kid who died and nobody did anything about it… I think I'd go stark raving mad. It was bad enough…" She grabbed her shoe and started shoving it back on. "Well, if that's all you need," she said brightly, "I'll just go make some calls."

"What was bad enough?" I asked, looking up from my notes. I couldn't help the question; it spilled out before I thought.

"My brother dying. He was twelve. It was horrible." She grabbed her purse. "So if you don't need anything, I'll just be off then." With a quick wave, she was out the door before I had a chance to say goodbye.

I was stunned. She'd met my sister, I thought, sitting with my hands lying limply on my desk, but I knew nothing about her family. How could a person talk so much, yet reveal so little, about her own background?

That evening, I found my way to the Jacobses' home on the west side of town. They lived only a few blocks from West Hospital, which turned out to not be a coincidence.

"Yes, I work at the hospital doing transfusions," Arthur

Jacobs said after shaking my hand and offering me a seat in their small but comfortable living room. His wife perched next to him on a wooden chair that looked like it had seen better days. She had a careworn face and a nervous smile.

"Ward told me you worked as a medic in the war," I said, sitting on a rather flat cushion. "I'd like to thank you for all you did."

"Transfusions were my specialty then as well," he said, taking a seat and clasping his hands on his knee. "I learned the trade in France, you could say. Did you lose someone?"

"A much older brother," I said, taking out the autophone. "I like to think that someone like you was there with him in the end. You have a kind face."

"Well, thank you," he said. His wife squeezed his hand. "Rosalie said that you had some questions for us, and that Thomas is a friend of yours as well?"

Busy programming the autophone, I paused a moment in perplexity. Then I laughed a little at myself. "Ward, yes. Yes, we work together sometimes. He likes to give me information for the *Franklin Journal,* where I work as a reporter."

The blood drained from Arthur's face. Rosalie looked at him with a strained expression.

"What would you like to know, exactly?" she whispered. At almost the same time, they both looked at the corner behind me. Feeling odd, I glanced back and saw a normal sized bookcase with knick-knacks and books jumbled comfortably together on the shelves.

We all looked back at one another.

"Well," I said, hitting record on the autophone, "there's a strange sickness over on Oak Hill; perhaps you've heard about it?"

Arthur shook his head, but Rosalie nodded.

"When I spoke to Ward about it, he said that your son suffered from something similar. I was wondering if you could tell me more about it. Please don't feel beholden to speak about it if you do not wish to do so."

Rosalie twined her skirt around her fingers, not looking at me. Arthur was frowning a little, as if thinking.

"He was so young," Rosalie said finally. "So young. He was never very well. I wasn't supposed to be able to have a child, and when I finally did, he had a hard life. Arthur did what he could, but his war training didn't prepare him for chronic illnesses." She turned just slightly so that their knees were touching. Arthur was gazing up behind me again. I itched to turn around but ignored the feeling, taking notes instead. "We saw several doctors, and then something changed for the worse. He had always been sickly, but suddenly his health deteriorated much more quickly than it should have done. At first we thought it was influenza. He coughed and had stomach pain and other similar ailments. Arthur always knew something else was going on. He gave him several blood transfusions, but…" She glanced at him again and stopped, as if waiting: either for him to continue where she left off or for permission to do so herself. I realized I was studying them with narrowed eyes and tried to relax my expression.

"It wasn't enough," Arthur said. "He would get better and then worse again." He was gripping his knees now, and when he made eye contact, I got the distinct idea he was trying to communicate more than he could say aloud. "We never found out what the disease was."

Rosalie caught his eye, and for a moment, I knew they were having a conversation from which I was barred. A prickly shiver crawled about on my neck.

I cleared my throat. "Ward said that others in your neighborhood were also sick. That was here in this neighborhood?"

They turned back to me. "No. We lived on the south end then," Arthur said. A grandfather clock down the hall bonged, and I jumped a little.

"Arthur started a special blood transfusion department in the West Hospital after Matthew died," Rosalie said, her eyes boring into me. What was she trying to tell me? My pen seemed inert, useless. There was a message I was not receiving.

"And your neighbors — they had the same symptoms?"

They nodded yes. "The sickness went away," Rosalie said. "But Matthew had already died." Her face hardened. "He was the only one. All the rest got well again."

Arthur's head was in his hands. When he raised it to look at me, I saw an old man still young. What weren't they telling me? The air was thick with held-back information. I felt that if I could simply find the right question, I could cut through it to find the truth.

"You thought it was the water?"

"No," Arthur said, too quickly. "That was never a concern." When I looked up from my notes, he was nodding at me, and Rosalie was studying my face desperately. I tapped my pen against my thigh.

"It wasn't? I must have heard wrong."

"Yes, you must have." They were both shaking their heads now.

I stared at them. "Perhaps the cases are not related then," I said carefully. "Sero Electric is claiming that the water is polluted." They were nodding again, emphatically. I continued. "But the generator from Panrose that they accused is not the problem." They shook their heads.

"A strange case," Arthur said. "But if it's something in the water, the similar symptoms must be purely coincidental."

The crawly feeling on my neck felt like a vise now. Their behavior suggested only one thing to me, and I didn't even know how it could be possible. Someone was listening to our conversation, someone who didn't want me to link these two cases.

I tried to laugh normally as I jotted a sentence on my

paper. "I just thought of something our friend Ward always says."

Clenching each other's hands, they stared at me through fear-darkened expressions.

"Life is full of coincidences." I smiled at them.

They relaxed visibly and then bent to read the paper I passed to them.

Tell me where to go next.

"I'm so sorry we couldn't be more help," Rosalie said, sounding genuinely sorry. I wondered how long she had been a consummate actress in her own home. She ushered me to the door.

"Please don't think of it," I said, pressing her hand. "I get false leads all the time. I really am sorry to have brought up such a painful subject. You must forgive me."

"We left it behind long ago," Arthur said. He took my hand with a grip that was so urgent it almost hurt. "These things happen. Sometimes you just have to let it go." He held my palm a moment longer and then released me, leaving something in my hand. "Be careful," he called as I walked down their front steps. "We get some tough guys around here sometimes. I'd have Thomas meet you if I were you."

"Thanks!" I called back, waving. "I'll do that."

When I turned the corner and was out of sight of their house, I took out my morsie to make good on my promise. Only after sending the message did I pull the slip of paper that Arthur had passed me from my sleeve. It contained only four words:

Samuel Ragoczy, West Hospital

I tore it into tiny pieces and let them speckle the muddy water of the gutter as I walked on, shaking with leftover fear — and excitement.

It had finally happened: I'd caught the scent of the Hunt.

8

"You must have flown here," I told Ward as he caught up to me two blocks down from the Jacobses' house. "Don't you have crimes to solve?"

"You're rather jaunty," he said, eying me shrewdly. His long legs were eating up the distance between us and my apartment. I slowed so we could talk longer. He agreeably matched my pace. "And yes, I do, in fact, but I'm efficient. What did you find out?"

"I don't know yet." I tapped my notes excitedly. "But you've given me the key. The Jacobses are being watched… or listened to… You should have seen how jumpy they were." I smoothed my hair with my hand. "And they kept looking at the bookcase behind me as if it were going to jump forward and bite them. Arthur gave me the name 'Samuel Ragoczy' at the West Hospital when I asked him where to go next. We wrote that part on paper because they obviously couldn't answer my questions aloud. They kept saying one thing and indicating another with body language." I shivered. "I really can't tell you how creepy it was."

"Audi-spies," Ward muttered. He noticed my quizzical expression and explained. "Maybe this Ragoczy uses a listening device called an audi-spy. They're new to the market, very expensive, but we used them in the war. They can transmit over very long distances and would be perfect for listening in on people you don't trust."

"So they must have figured it out," I breathed. "They as good as told me the sickness was in the water." Massaging my neck, I sighed impatiently. "I hope Dr. Laining gets back to me soon. I left her the samples this afternoon. When she does, we'll know for certain what's in the water… though I still won't know how it got there. I'm certain the Jacobses know, however. Maybe I could meet with them in public and get them to answer questions candidly."

We stopped at the curb, watching automobiles chug by. I could still feel my heart pounding the rhythm of the Hunt in my chest. The sun was low in the sky now; I sensed the crawly fingers on my neck again as I remembered Arthur's warning.

"If they didn't offer to meet in public when you contacted them, I doubt they'll be able to now," Ward said, his forehead creasing in deep grooves. "Now that you've spoken with them, if someone is keeping tabs on them, they'll be even more careful now. They may be watched; you may be followed. Someone might even be watching their morsies."

We walked across the empty intersection; I threw a glance surreptitiously over my shoulder as we did so. A businessman shoved past us, typing into his morsie, headed toward the hospital, which sparked my memory.

"Rosalie said that Arthur started working for the hospital after their son died." I turned to Ward and saw that he was already looking at me with inscrutable eyes. "What?"

"He wasn't working there when I was investigating the case, or while we were still in contact," he said. "But that is where the boy was taken when he was dying."

"But they lived on the south end then," I said, checking my notes. "Wouldn't they go to East Hospital?"

"Yes," he said. "But West Hospital is the same distance

from there as East, and it's less expensive, as it does not cater to Park residents."

My morsie dinged. True to Felicity's nature, the message was far longer than most morsies I received.

<SEVERAL MAJOR SERO INVESTORS STOP ONLY ONE REALLY BIG ONE STOP SPELLING IS HOPELESS STOP SAMUEL RAGOKSEE STOP SOUNDED RUSSIAN STOP NEVER HEARD OF HIM STOP OWNS 20 PERCENT OF COMPANY STOP>

The crawly feeling danced tiptoe down my spine.

"Ward," I whispered. He read the paper. The shutters dropped over his eyes. He handed it back, and I tore it up as I had its brother, my shaking fingers sprinkling the evidence in a trash bucket outside a shop.

"From your new assistant?" he asked finally. I nodded. A thought struck me, and I typed a new message to Felicity.

<DO YOU HAVE FRIENDS WORKING AT WEST HOSPITAL STOP CHECK HIS NAME THERE STOP>

"Let me know when you hear from the professor," Ward said as I stowed the morsie again. "We'll need to open a criminal investigation if she finds evidence of purposeful contamination." We wove through a rowdy group of young people, and on the other side of the merriment, Ward took my arm to navigate me around some dog droppings. "Can I get you to promise that you won't go places alone until this is finished?"

"I can try not to," I said, endeavoring to keep my voice light even as my heart thumped from his warning — and perhaps from his kindness. "But I've investigated dangerous stories before. I'll be careful."

"I know about those dangerous stories," he muttered. "And I know better than to think that going in pairs is a guarantee of safety." We must have been remembering the same moment: the one that still haunted my nights when I least expected it, the one where he fell two stories after being electrocuted while shielding me. He checked his morsie before continuing. "But I also know that the chances of an attack on two people are less than the chances of an attack on one. I advise you not to gamble on the odds." The night was not chilly, but I found myself shivering again. "We don't know who this Ragoczy is yet, and until we do, it's best not to take any chances. It concerns me that I've never heard his name before."

"Especially when he must be rather connected," I added, trying not to look over my shoulder again. I was concentrating on fighting the flashbacks that flooded my mind: the high, high scaffolding, the masked pursuer, the torment in the murderer's eyes after he chose not to kill me, instead, escaping another way with a sound that would never, ever be erased from my ears.

"It's Felicity again," I said in a shaking voice as my morsie dinged.

<NO STOP BUT I HAVE A FRIEND WHOSE COUSIN WORKS THERE STOP I SENT HER A MESSAGE STOP IS HE A DOCTOR STOP IF HE IS I CLAIM FIRSTIES STOP DOCTORS ARE SOOO ROMANTIC STOP>

A startled laugh choked out of my tight throat. "You know, It's very effective to have an assistant who knows everyone in the city," I told Ward, trying to keep my voice from wavering. "She's checking to see what Ragoczy does at the hospital."

"Good. Tell her to be careful, too," he said. He smiled a bit grimly. "Though she seemed pretty savvy."

"As opposed to me?"

"Yes," he said, but his eyes were warm when I scowled at him. "Most people may have forgotten where you came from, but I do not."

"What you're saying is that someone high born can never be smart enough to live safely in this dangerous city." Irritation prickled under my skin.

"No, Miss Harper, I am not." He raised an eyebrow at me. "But you jumped very quickly to that conclusion. Are you still sensitive about your upbringing?"

"No," I said, too hastily. "I simply don't appreciate being thought stupid."

He shook his head. "You, of all people, know that I find you far from stupid. And now you've tricked me into complimenting you. Here we are." He took off his hat and used it to point to my apartment door, which we had reached without me noticing. I was still irritated, though mollified to an extent. As I took my key from my pocket, I turned to him, remembering something else from the Jacobses.

"They said the people in their neighborhood eventually got better," I told him. "Why poison water only for a time? How could one benefit from that?"

"Find out what Ragoczy does at the hospital," Ward said, replacing his hat. "Lunch tomorrow?"

"On Cod Street," I said, giving in. "Have a good night."

"You as well." I almost missed his smile as I turned to enter my apartment. "Sweet dreams."

Some people would say that flippantly, I thought, as I waved before closing and locking the door. But Ward knew — he understood what dreams were like after living through what we had. He understood better than I did, I admitted to myself, putting on the water to boil for tea. Suddenly sorry for my harsh words, I turned and stepped outside.

"Stay for tea?" I yelled down the street to his back.

Popping back inside before my neighbors could see who had yelled, I pulled out two mugs with an ironic smile on my face as I considered what my father would think of me inviting a man inside to have tea with me — and at dusk no less.

9

In my dreams that night, I was again in my kitchen, pondered soulfully as I poured hot water over rose tea leaves. Ward's and my conversation must have impacted me, because even in my sleep, I was reflecting that I may have been born into a privileged position, but I was thankful for my background instead of ashamed, because my previous life lent a broader perspective, and therefore gratitude, to my current life. I appreciate the simple things, the freedom, the honesty.

I was musing over this and puzzling over why my kitchen looked different from normal when coarse hands tightened around my throat.

I thrashed and found myself bound, paralyzed, and fell backwards, where Gaines knelt, throttling the life breath out of me. Dr. Sylvester appeared to stand over us, gloating. I panicked, the air from my lungs depleting. Then I heard Felicity scream as if being tortured. There she was, lying beside me, having just fallen through my ceiling, her chest blasted open as the others I'd seen too many times last year…

I woke already standing, my fists balled, sweat running rivulets down my face and chest. Trembling to the point of swaying, I collapsed back onto my bed, then jolted upwards again to fetch a towel. Sponging away the sweaty remnants of the dream, I breathed deeply, concentrating first on the sensation of the rough braided rug under my feet, then the wisp of nightdress against my legs, the biting cold of the water I was scrubbing onto my stomach, and the life-full feeling of my breath expanding and emptying my chest. "What do you see?" Ward would have asked me. "What do you hear? Grasp the moment; let go the dream."

I hung the towel and opened my palms, following his instructions in my mind.

It was morning.

I was awake.

I was safe.

It was time for breakfast, time for tea.

It was time to think about what I would do today.

As I sat in my beloved, rickety chair, finding the impression in the cushion that enveloped my form just so, I set aside my steaming mug, pulled out my piano-miniature, and thought back to what Ward and I had discussed after I'd invited him in last evening. My fingers coaxed "Let the Rest of the World Go By" from the keys, and my body slowly relaxed as I remembered.

We had discarded the earlier conversation about my upbringing; Ward was ever a good sport that way.

Instead, we talked about his mob case that had just hit the presses with Daniels' name proudly printed under it. Ward was only semi-disgusted with the story, which I considered a win for the *Journal*. He told me the full version as we sipped and ate the remains of stale cookies from my tin.

"Do you think you'll ever fully stop them?" I'd asked, feeling the despondency that I always did when speaking about the mob. "They call to mind the hydra in old Greek stories: one head always rising up to replace the one that was destroyed."

"I like to think it doesn't matter," Ward said, surprising me. "Criminals don't change unless they're reformed by God himself. The mob is just one example. What really matters is that I do all I can to keep folks safe. I'd go mad if I thought I could do more. So I just do what I can."

"And better than most," I murmured into my tea. He smiled.

"It's the same for you. You can't tell every story in this city, but you tell the ones that people most need to hear; wouldn't you agree?"

I nodded. "We do our part."

"That's all that's required."

I wondered now, standing shivering in my kitchen, clutching an old towel, what my part would end up being in this story of the sick water. Would I uncover a poisoner? Perhaps save people like my brother-in-law from Matthew's fate? Or would I simply tell their tragedy, the truth of what one hydra head accomplished before it was chopped to bits?

I felt like chopping up more than one head before I reached my desk that morning. Recovering from my nightmare had left me jumpy and irritable. I stepped in horse manure twice while looking over my shoulder for pursuers. I hadn't caught breakfast with Diggory and Rufus since they met Felicity, and now I worried for the millionth time what Diggory was doing while roaming the streets. A trio of early morning drunks catcalled me when I was almost to the *Journal*, and my fingers were itching for my boot knives when Felicity came running toward me with a bright smile stretched across her face.

"Oh boys, go home and sleep it off," she laughed, shooing the drunks away. "You're sassing a public figure!" Leaving them to stumble away wondering what she meant, she grabbed my arm and hauled me inside before I could do anything rash.

"I should get Ward to raid that speakeasy on Seventh Street," I growled.

"You know they'd just move it next week, and then where would we get our morning entertainment?" She laughed. "I've got news." She plunked me down in my chair and handed me a donut. "My friend's cousin doesn't work at the hospital anymore, but she sent me her boss's number, and I got what we wanted. Ragoczy is the hospital manager." She leaned on my desk, shifting one hip out and crossing her arms. "What do you think of that?" While I digested this, she pouted her lips quizzically and cocked her head. "No really, what do you think of that? Why are we interested in a Sero investor who manages a hospital?"

With a start, I remembered I hadn't told her about the Jacobses yet. I rubbed my temple and motioned her closer.

"When I went to the Jacobses' yesterday, they indicated that they knew how their son was poisoned. It was from the water. Someone's spying on them — probably with some sort of audio technology — Ward knows about it. When I asked where to go next, Mr. Jacobs told me 'Samuel Ragoczy at West Hospital.'" I sat back in my chair, suddenly weary.

"So…" Felicity wiggled, sending a pen toppling to the floor. "Is he the problem? Or the solution?"

"We don't know yet," I said, retrieving the pen peevishly.

"Well, that's our next step. I can't date a poisoner. It's too difficult keeping up a relationship in prison."

Lord help me, I thought, gazing at the ceiling.

She eyed me, tapping her pen against her magenta lips. "What's up?"

"What do you mean?" I pulled a paper toward me to outline a plan for the day.

"You're not Ginnie Harper, star reporter for the *Franklin Journal*, mender of wrongs and proclaimer of truth today." She kicked her patent leather pumps and quirked a small grin. "You're Miss Harper, eyes of storm clouds and snapper of necks."

I glanced up, ever startled by her insightfulness. "You couldn't be obtuse for just one morning, could you?"

"Oh, never. It's not in my job description. Talk to Mac. But really — I thought you'd be excited that we have a genuine lead at last!"

I took a deep breath. It didn't help either of us — or the story — to have me distracted and irritated. I let out the breath and expelled my dark mood with it as best I could. "I am… I think… I just didn't sleep well."

"Hmm," she said, eying me and the paper that I was numbering. "Well then. Let's make our plan and go. I've got somewhere to show you."

Deciding not to ask for details, I accordingly laid out our schedule for the day.

"I'm going to go through the old newspaper records from five years ago when the other neighborhood was poisoned. You'll do more digging on Ragoczy. What else does he invest in? You can also call the hospital and set up a meeting with him."

"Perfect," she said, hopping off the desk and grabbing the phone. "Set aside an hour before dinner. Right there." She jabbed five o'clock on my appointment calendar and ran to a quiet corner, her absurdly green purse bouncing against her hips as she went.

Bringing a pad of paper with me, I went through the hall past the Tips Desk and down to the records room that we affectionately called the Morgue. The old stairs creaked as I gripped the splintery railing and descended into the basement. My feet left dusty footprints on the weathered wood. Hardly anyone came down here besides the filing secretary. The last time I had was at least three years ago, looking for information on an uncaught murderer when he started killing again. It was a long job, thumbing through years of daily newspapers.

I found the section categorizing newspapers from five years ago and carried the boxes to an old dusty table, squinting through the smeary folds with precious little aid from the dreary light of the switch lamp next to the table.

After ten minutes, two false hopes with influenza stories, and five bouts of sneezing fits, I turned a page and found a reference to an epidemic on the south side. Matthew's death was not mentioned (it must not have happened yet), but Mr. Jacobs was the star of the article: he was portrayed as a noble father with an invalid son, championing for his family and community against the oppression of bad water polluted by the rich. I noticed several references from *The Jungle* and shook my head with a smile. The reporter, a certain Ezra Longhorn, must have been following the socialist cause when this happened. He focused on testimonials and quotes from people in the Jacobses' neighborhood. While I appreciated his humanitarian angle, I was frustrated that he hadn't included more facts on the illness or timelines of what had happened. Groaning over the writing style, I landed on something that made me stop in my tracks two papers later.

According to this small story on page seven, a Mr. Benjamin Gaines of the south end had died of arsenic poisoning. I stared at the story. Gaines. Yes, here it said that he was the co-owner of Sero Electric. There was no mention of the epidemic. The reporter was apparently just writing the obituary. I squinted at the reporter's name: Peter Smith.

Beating a rhythm against my thigh, I thought through the staff upstairs. Yes, there was a Peter Smith. I didn't report to him so we had no interaction, but I remembered the nameplate on a desk near the advertising department.

Quickly, I flipped through the rest of the year's papers but found nothing on the epidemic. Ezra had apparently lost interest when there was nothing new to tell. He also was the reporter on a corruption story that spanned several papers after this — he must have been sidetracked. I took the paper that had Gaines' obituary in it and jogged up the stairs to the advertising department to find his desk. Behind it sat an older gentleman with mussed white hair and a potbelly.

"Can I help you?" Smith said in a deep voice, sounding genuinely inquisitive.

"Excuse me," I said, "I'm Ginnie Harper. I'm looking into an illness caused by bad water on the Hill."

"Ah yes," he said, waving me to an empty chair that he took from another desk and pulled up beside him. He shifted his chair to face me. "I've been following that one. I run the ad department, but I read the whole *Journal* every day to catch Mac's mistakes." He winked at me. "What can I do for you?"

I laid the crinkly newspaper on his desk and pointed to the obituary. "You can tell me more about this man, if you remember anything. I'm assuming he's a relation to the Gaines who owns Sero Electric? The one claiming the hydroelectric generator is poisoning the Hill residents?"

"Ah," he said. "Now I see the connection." He pushed his glasses up on his nose and read the story. "I don't remember much, but I remember a bit of hushing that went on." When I raised my eyebrows, he shook his head. "It's different now at the *Journal*. Mac is belligerent, but he doesn't take bribes. The last owner was… another story, shall we say. Quite a… character. Yes, this Benjamin Gaines is the brother of the current Gaines. They owned Sero together. When I did the story, I talked to the deceased's wife and doctor. The wife was appropriately tearful, but I always wondered about her. The doctor, a fellow with a Greekish sounding name, Xavier, I think, told me — after the autopsy showed arsenic poisoning — that he had been treating Mr. Gaines for syphilis with the new arsenic pills. I remember being shocked by that, but he assured me they were very safe and quite effective as well. The wife maintained that Mr. Gaines had been forgetful with his pills and accidentally took more than he should have while she was away with her family. The coroner ruled it an accidental overdose, and the syphilis part was hushed. I was allowed to print the arsenic poisoning. It created quite a buzz. You don't see arsenic poisonings now like you did a hundred years ago. Doctors don't usually even consider it. That barbaric time is past, thankfully."

"Did neither of them mention anything about the sickness going around in that area? There was a boy who died from polluted water around the same time."

He shook his head. "Sounds familiar, but I wasn't covering that story. I'm not aware that there was any relation, as this was definitively arsenic poisoning. The coroner was very clear on that point."

"You said you wondered about the wife," I pressed. "Why?"

He sat back in his chair and peered at me thoughtfully. Around us, the hum of the department continued, though I caught a few curious looks thrown our way. "Have you noticed, Miss Harper, the way you learn to read people in this business? The many interviews, the many lies?"

I nodded, thinking of Gaines rubbing his fingers and thigh.

"I was a reporter for nineteen years before I moved up here," he said. "I still notice the little ticks that show when people feel differently than they are saying. Or the ones that show anxiety." He pointed to my fingers tapping out a Beethoven piece on my knee. "How long have you done that?"

I stopped and looked at my fingers. I hadn't even noticed I was doing it. "Oh. Ah… several months, I think." I flushed. I had started playing pieces on my knee the week after the Blaster Murders ended.

Smith nodded genially. "Our bodies do what our subconscious directs, and a canny reporter can pick up on those things. I sensed relief and fear in the wife even though she talked as if she were grief stricken. That stuck with me — which is probably why I remember this little paragraph out of the thousands I wrote." He pointed to the article with a gnarled finger. "I felt sorry for the fellow, not knowing what really happened to him."

"Stifling the true story leaves a mark," I murmured as I refolded the newspaper.

"Yes," he said, lacing his fingers on his belly and staring vaguely around at the bustling room. "I suppose you're right. I told myself for months that there was nothing else I could do, but one always wonders, wouldn't you say?"

"Yes. Always." I rose slowly, straightening my vest. "Do you remember anything else that might be helpful to me? I'm looking for anything at all."

He took his time thinking, which I appreciated. "I found it interesting that the wife married one of the Sero board members soon after her husband's death. I covered the wedding; she seemed nervous to see me there. Her former brother-in-law, who you mentioned, spent a lot of time whining at the reception, talking about how the company was going to the dogs without his brother." He barked out a short, scratchy laugh. "I never liked Gaines."

"Thank you," I said, intrigued. I scraped the chair back to its original desk and stepped over to shake his hand. "You've been most helpful."

An hour later, Felicity's phone skills were showing their value. We had a meeting scheduled with Ragoczy at one o'clock, and she'd found that he had fingers in several businesses in town, including Sero Electric, Hammer's Coal, Heavenly Sweets Bakery, Laier Shipping, Achman's Orchards, Forman's Pharmacy, and Nelly's Laundry. I avoided asking Felicity how she got such detailed records, suspecting her friend at the bank. However, she proved more resourceful than I'd guessed, volunteering instead that when she'd called his secretary for the meeting, she'd then asked to speak with his personal records person.

"You mean his financial secretary?" the woman had asked disapprovingly. "He works for a private firm."

Once Felicity found that number, she'd called there.

"I'm just such an admirer of Mr. Ragoczy's business strategy," she'd gushed. (I could picture her batting her eyelashes at the man, though they were only connected by the phone.) "But I'm really calling to settle a bet. My coworker argues that a single investment in an up-and-coming company, like Panrose Electric for example, is a much better move than putting money into several different companies. I disagree, don't you? I'd heard that Mr. Ragoczy agrees with me, but when I brought up his name, my coworker laughed in my face, saying he only invests in one company! Sero Electric! So I said I'd prove him wrong. He is wrong, isn't he?"

"My dear young woman! Miss Jones, you said your name is? Oh, Felicity? A very pretty name, my dear… yes! You are absolutely right. Any financial man worth his salt will tell you to diversify! Why, Mr. Ragoczy has money all over the city!"

"Just in electric companies? My coworker says that's where the money is."

"Oh no, indeed, no, no. Diversification means all sorts of businesses! For example, Mr. Ragoczy is wise enough to invest in a bakery and a laundry! These very practical businesses are what make our city what it is!"

"My friend will never believe that. But perhaps you can't tell me the names of these places. I would understand…"

"Won't believe you? My dear girl, you need to find other friends!"

And then he'd told her the name of every business. By the end of the conversation, he'd hinted that she could come interview for a secretary position for him.

"This is a little late," I told her, trying to keep the admiration out of my voice, "but part of being transparent is telling your source that you work for the newspaper."

"Such a shame you informed me of that rule that too late," Felicity said in mock regret.

I told her what I'd learned about Gaines' brother and found her interest gratifying.

"Do you think he suspected poisoned water killed his brother?" Felicity asked, perching herself on my desk again. "And that's why he's so dead set on framing Panrose with the Hill water?"

"It certainly makes you wonder, doesn't it?"

My morsie dinged twice. I pulled it out to find a message from Laining and another from Ward.

<RAGOCZY HAS MONEY IN EVERYTHING INCLUDING HAMMERS COAL STOP HAMMERS IS SEROS FUEL SUPPLIER STOP HAVE YOU HEARD FROM LAINING STOP>

It was a relief to know that Ward had the same information as Felicity, as he (hopefully) would have checked in a more ethical manner.

"Felicity," I said, realizing the import of his message. "Hammer's Coal supplies Sero Electric. Ragoczy has double interest in Sero's business gains."

Her eyes gleamed. "What's the other one say?"

I held my breath as I checked Laining's message with Felicity peering over my shoulder.

<WATER HAS RELATIVELY HIGH TRACES OF

ARSENIC STOP SENDING FULL RESULTS VIA MAIL
STOP I WILL CHECK WATER AT SOURCE THIS
AFTERNOON TO NOTIFY CITY OF
CONTAMINATION STOP I TOLD CITY OFFICIALS
TO WARN HILL RESIDENTS NOT TO DRINK TAP
WATER>

10

"Arsenic," Felicity and I said at the same time.
"But that was what killed Gaines' brother," I said,
taken aback.

"What if…" she stopped. "What if he was already taking
the pills, and then someone poisoned his neighborhood water
with arsenic — and that's what made him overdose?"

"Yes," I said. "And Matthew died from the arsenic water
even when it wasn't enough to kill anyone else because he was
already sickly. Felicity, please find out everything you can
about arsenic poisoning. I've got to get information to Chastity
for Edwin. Thank goodness Laining notified the Hill residents,
so they'll quit drinking their water! Can you imagine?" My
mind raced with implications.

"Right away!" She gave me that ridiculous salute again,
but I hardly noticed.

Someone was poisoning the water with arsenic, which also
happened five years ago. Did Gaines know? Is that why he was
pursuing this so doggedly? But then why not reveal the
genuine problem: arsenic? Why talk about filters and
contaminants? Unless… unless he not only knew, but he was a
conspirator. He hadn't killed his brother, had he?

I caught my breath and stood, tapping my thigh in agitation. I needed to call Ward.

Pinching a phone from the desk next to mine, I ignored its owner's protests and rung up Ward, who answered after the first ring.

"It's arsenic," I said. "There's arsenic in the water. And get this, five years ago, Gaines' brother who lived on the south end died of arsenic poisoning, thought to be an overdose of his syphilis treatment. What if the Jacobses found that someone was putting arsenic in the water, and that's what killed Matthew, too?"

"So we have evidence of an intentional poisoning now," Ward said. "That's enough for me to open a case. I'll call the Hill precinct. We're lucky you've done most of the research already. Did you find anything else on Ragoczy?"

"We have an interview with him at one o'clock. You can tag along if you'd like, but I think we might get more out of him in a first interview if the police are not represented. I'll record it." I stopped and held my breath for a moment in excitement. "Ward, do you think these two cases are related?"

"Jacobs seemed to think so. It's very interesting. We need to find out more without getting them in trouble. What's your angle for interviewing Ragoczy?"

I covered the receiver with my hand and jogged over to my assistant. "Felicity!" I hissed.

"What?" She covered her phone, too.

"What did you tell Ragoczy's secretary for the interview?" I held my phone up to her face.

"Um, since he's a major investor in Sero, we want to know what he thinks about these claims — especially since he manages a hospital that treats the Hill residents."

I gave her a thumbs up and scurried back to my desk. "Did you get that?"

"Yes. I think it would be best if I stayed away this time, as you said. I'd like the recording as soon as you can get it to me. Meet at Mel's Diner after you're done?"

"Sure," I said, jotting it down on my calendar. "Is there anything you'd like me to ask him?"

There was a pause. "Follow your gut, Miss Harper. See you soon."

I hung up and immediately started writing questions on my pad of paper. If Ragoczy was involved, how would I get him to admit it?

Five minutes later, Felicity interrupted my musings with a list of bodily ailments.

"Abdominal pain, headaches, nausea, vomiting, loose bowels, and skin discoloring," she recited, bouncing up and down on her toes. "Arsenic can also cause vertigo. That's why Edwin couldn't walk on his own! He was dizzy! The doctor *also* said that long exposure to it can give you a perpetually sore throat." She wiggled her eyebrows at me. "Remember how he kept clearing his throat? If he was right about the timeline, then he's been drinking arsenic water for over a year!"

"Is there a cure?"

"They can get blood transfusions. That's about all the doctors can do."

I sat back, breathless. "Can you write all that down? For Edwin? I'll tell Chastity to get their doctor to check for arsenic." I grabbed my morsie and started typing furiously. There was so much to do, and the information was pouring in like a waterfall. My body was humming with energy. We were so close to the solution that I could taste it like a metallic twinge on my tongue.

"Felicity," I said, checking my watch. "We have a few hours before the meeting. We need to check Gaines' and Sero's financial records to see if we can find any trace of the arsenic. The poisoner must get it from somewhere. Call Professor Laining and see if she knows where one could buy arsenic in large amounts. No — I'll do that. You work your magic on some more accounting workers. See if Ragoczy's man knows anything. Be careful, though."

"Careful?" she laughed, the Hunt reflected in her eyes, too. "I'll be more careful than a snail crossing the road in front of the Orchid House at midnight. Give me an hour and I'll have what we need!"

I shook my head, still feeling the rush of excitement, and rang up Laining as soon as Felicity was gone.

"Professor Laining? Hi, it's Ginnie Harper from the *Franklin* again. I really appreciate your help with the water samples. You're sure that it's arsenic in all of them?"

"All except the control sample from the university here," she answered cheerfully. "Almost an exact percentage in each one. I would say that it's enough to make a person sick over a long period of time, but probably not enough to kill anyone. I assume that's exactly what you were looking for?"

"It was, yes," I said, smiling. "And I have another question. You wouldn't happen to know where one could acquire that much arsenic, would you? It would take copious amounts to poison a neighborhood's water supply, wouldn't it?"

"Oh yes. The arsenic in this water was a ratio of thirty parts arsenic to one billion parts water. Less than ten parts of arsenic to one billion parts of water is safe. Practically, they'd do it every week to keep people sick. To buy it in bulk without arousing suspicion? Let me think."

I heard a rustle of papers and what sounded like the dull thump of books bumping one another on a shelf.

"Currently, one of the biggest uses of arsenic is in agriculture," she said. "It's also in beauty products — don't worry, not enough to hurt you… hopefully. Medicines, too. I believe the most effective treatment for syphilis is a form of arsenic. I have a colleague here who has worked on that." She paused. "One wouldn't order large quantities for that, unfortunately. Only a very tiny amount is used. Maybe in production?"

I looked at the list I'd written as she talked. "Agriculture?"

"Oh yes, it's a pesticide. Very effective against apple worms."

My eyes fell on the list of Ragoczy's investments, and something clicked in my head. "So… an orchard would order a large quantity every year?"

"A commercial orchard? Oh my, yes." She paused as the idea took hold of my mind. "You sound like you're on to something. I won't pester you, but I will scan the next *Franklin* for your article. Will you be quoting me?"

"Would you like me to?"

"Couldn't hurt my ego."

I chuckled. "Oh, one more thing, if you don't mind, Professor. Are there other names for arsenic? If I'm looking for it in financial records, what would I find?"

"Ah, yes. It has different aliases, if you will. Here we are: Arsenate, Arsenic Pentoxide, Arsenic Trichloride, Arsenic Trioxide, Arsenite, Atomic Number Thirty-Three, Fowler's Solution, Sodium Arsenite, Trichlorure d'Arsenic — oh no, wait, that one's just Trichloride in French." She laughed. "Of course, it's also called ratsbane — rat poison, you know."

I read back what she'd said and added the ones I'd missed. "Thank you so much. Your help has been invaluable."

"You're too kind. Glad to be of help. I'll let you know if the water is contaminated at the source. Keep in touch — it's been lovely."

I hung up and circled Achman's Orchards with a thick, bold line. Pressing invisible piano keys on my desk as I thought, I wondered how to get Gaines' financial records. If I could manage it, it might be a simple thing to find our arsenic source. I looked up and saw Felicity coming toward me, looking curiously at my fingers playing a concerto on my desk. I stopped and put my hands in my lap.

"You don't happen to know anyone at Achman's Orchards, do you?" I asked with an ironic smile. If this worked, it would be uncanny.

"No — where's that?"

"It's a short train ride north," I said. "What did you find?"

"Nothing." She looked dejected. "I only chatted up one person so far. He was useless." She picked up her pocketbook from my desk and headed for the door. "I'm going to Sero's. Gaines isn't in, and his accountant sounded like a good lead, but only in person. I can't charm his type over the phone."

I decided not to ask what she meant.

"Look out for anything from Achman's, won't you? If we're on the right track with Ragoczy and Gaines, I have a hunch that the arsenic may come from there."

She looked befuddled.

"Arsenic is used as a pesticide," I explained. "Here, take this list of arsenic aliases with you."

"Poison on fruit. Creepy," she muttered on her way out the door.

Not wanting to waste any time, I jotted down a few questions, and when I couldn't think of any more, I called Ward again.

"Professor Laining said that the poisoner would need to add arsenic to the water weekly in order to keep the people sick without killing them. Have you thought of posting a lookout near the generator?"

"I have. In fact, I just got out of a meeting regarding that very issue." He sighed. "The chief isn't thrilled about it, but if it's only for a week, he might be more amenable."

"Catching the culprit red-handed would be very helpful," I said. "Just one good tug on this knot could unravel the whole scheme."

"We simply need to find the right place to pull," he agreed. I heard papers shuffling on his side, and his voice sounded muffled for a moment, as if he were holding the receiver with his shoulder. "Ragoczy may be that key. If you can get a confession from him, I'll send you a personal thank-you letter from the precinct. I know all the night shift lookouts would sign it."

I laughed, running a hand through my hair. "We'll do what I can. I'm feeling a bit intimidated, though. No one knows much about this man, and yet he has fingers in every pie in Luxity!"

"If he turns out to be our culprit and you can't wring a confession out of him, we'll get him another way."

"Thanks," I said. "Sooner rather than later will suit me. I'll see you at Mel's."

The next hour and a half crawled by as I reviewed everything we had found out and double and triple checked my questions for Ragoczy. Every couple minutes I doubted myself: were we really on the right track? What if all these facts were just a collection of coincidences and I was wasting Felicity's and my time? Ward's catchphrase bubbled up in my mind, and I stifled a pleased snort. Surely he was right; surely what we'd gathered was far too much to be coincidence. And if Felicity could tie Ragoczy to the arsenic in some way, even just by investing money… I forced myself to sit down at my typewriter and get some work done.

I had a brief story written for tomorrow's paper by the time Felicity jogged up to our desk.

"The only weird shipment they get at Sero is an enormous case of apples…" her eyes shot wicked sparks, "from Achman's Orchards."

I clenched my fists in anticipation, sensing she wasn't finished.

"*And* it comes with a bag of Fowler's Solution. Double arsenic!"

I could hear Ward's voice in my head saying, "There are no coincidences." I almost whooped, and Felicity looked just as tickled as I was.

"That's right. It's a leukemia treatment, I think. The accountant said Gaines' doctor prescribed apples and Fowler's Solution when Gaines developed a health problem last year, so that must be how they're masking the shipments of poison." She rolled her eyes. "Apparently, he makes all his employees eat the apples, too. I love apples, but I think I'd refuse to eat them — just to spite him." She made a face. "Especially now that I know they're sprayed with arsenic."

"I think they spray the trees before the apples develop," I said absently, flipping through my notes and organizing them. "This accountant is an excellent source — you'll want to keep him." I clasped my hands together and looked at her. "Felicity, do you realize what this means?"

"Ragoczy invests in Achman's, Achman's sends arsenic to Gaines, Gaines poisons the water to frame Panrose, and Gaines and Ragoczy benefit." She ticked the names off on her fingers.

"This might be it." I nodded, feeling giddy with our new information. Then a thought struck me. "Who is Gaines' doctor? The one who prescribed the Fowler's Solution?"

"Um…" She screwed up her face, thinking back. "Dr. Xavier. Sounds exotic, like Greek, doesn't it?"

"It's Arabic, I believe," I said, shuffling excitedly back through papers I'd just organized to find the Gaines obituary.. "And more importantly, it's also… the doctor who prescribed Gaines' brother's syphilis pills and said he died of overdose." I triumphantly held up my notes from talking to Peter.

Felicity squealed.

"It's all coming together," I said, putting my hand over my mouth to muffle my own excitement.

"So we have concrete connections between Xavier, Gaines, Sero, Achman's, and Ragoczy," she said, drumming her colorful fingernails triumphantly on my desk.

"I don't know if they're concrete, but they're definitely

solid enough to ask some hard questions of some important peop-"

My morsie interrupted me with a message from Laining.

<SOURCE OF HILL WATER IS CLEAN STOP NO ARSENIC STOP> I read aloud to Felicity, who let out a whoop.

As we celebrated our breakthrough, our compositor, Sammy, came up behind Felicity with a grin.

"Caught yourselves a poisoner, yet, ladies?"

"Practically!" Felicity looked over her shoulder and batted her eyelashes at him. "You'll be laying out a front page for us soon — just wait!"

Sammy cupped his mouth and turned to the room at large. "Hear that, boys? The Oak Hill Poisoner is going down!"

Good-natured laughter rose from the room; they knew what it was like to have the scent of the Hunt. A few whistled and clapped as Felicity bowed, but I cut them off.

"We're not there yet!" I couldn't keep the smile from creeping over my face. "But we're certainly very close."

11

After I sent Ward a message with what we'd learned, Felicity and I left for lunch, discussing the questions I had written for Ragoczy. I ate robotically, too anxious about the meeting to taste my food, but one o'clock ticked into view quickly enough for us to hurry as we walked through the hospital doors and asked for the office of Samuel Ragoczy. A trim secretary dressed in a smart black suit led us to his door, which opened into a large, dark oak-paneled room with a window overlooking the city.

As we were ushered in and seated in front of the mammoth mahogany desk, I received the distinct impression that we were small and insignificant beings privileged to sit before a great and important man, who had deigned not to grace us with his presence yet. I raised my eyebrows as I scanned the expensive paintings and gold trim. If he went to all this trouble for intimidation, he must be hiding something big indeed. My fingers itched to discover it and write it down.

Felicity was clutching the autophone as Ragoczy entered the office after making us wait twenty minutes. I was startled to see him wheel in on a throne of a chair. The chair was controlled by a small device in his left hand. It was obviously designed by Morislav, and I added more dollar signs to his status in my head. He held a gold-tipped cane in his right hand, which he used to steady himself as he stood and transitioned to the tall chair behind his desk. The secretary who had earlier ushered us into his office hurried in with a machine that seemed to contain blood. With a practiced air, she attached thin tubes to bandaged areas on his arms and beefy neck. The scarlet liquid began transferring their contents through the tubes. The patient himself had the appearance of an impressive athlete who had gone to seed but was still trying to keep up appearances. His salt and pepper hair was thick, as was his full beard, which he kept nicely trimmed. His eyes, too, were black, and their piercing intelligence was deflected behind rectangular spectacles, which he now perched on his nose, peering down through them at us, mere bugs on his luscious office rug.

"Miss Harper and Miss Jacks," he said, nodding at us. I wondered how he knew which of us was which and raised my chin in response to the sense of power that he exuded from his very pores.

Naturally, Felicity was completely unaffected and gestured to the secretary as she exited the room. "A secretary *and* a nurse? You have quite a talented staff!"

He gave her a condescending look. "Yes, she is a very capable woman. I've made a habit of surrounding myself with exceptional people."

I settled into my chair, checking the questions in my notes with a bored air designed to combat his desire for control. "Mr. Ragoczy —"

"No, I'm sorry, but you can't record this interview, Miss Jacks," he interrupted, gesturing to Felicity, whose finger was poised over the autophone. "I don't allow recording devices in my office."

"No problem at all," I said, motioning to her to put it away. I caught the gleam in her eye: unbeknownst to him, as long as she was in the room and paying attention, we would have a perfect recall of the interview.

"May I take notes?" I asked, showing him my pencil and widening my eyes self-deprecatingly. "Just to jog my memory for later."

He rewarded me with an acquiescent smile. "Naturally, Miss Harper. One couldn't expect a person of your profession to put away her notebook for a friendly conversation."

"I'm never without it," I said, thinning my lips into a smile.

"I imagine," he said. "Now, what is this about? I believe you told my secretary that you want a quote from me as a Sero investor who also manages the Hill hospital." He clasped his hands and laid them on his desk in front of him. "We all know that is abhorrent nonsense. You want information on the sickness on the Hill, and you think I'm involved."

I looked up from my pad of paper and met his eyes.

When I was six, I was chased to exhaustion by a neighboring bulldog who escaped his owner. Finally, panting and terrified, I had given up, grabbed a branch, and turned around in helpless fury to face my attacker head on. The strident determination in my small, quivering body was what I saw now in Mr. Samuel Ragoczy of West Hospital. He knew. He knew we had him cornered. But he also knew he was the one with a stick.

Felicity rustled beside me, possibly getting ready to turn on the charm. I made the smallest possible gesture with my finger, which she miraculously caught and obeyed as I spoke.

"I did some research, Mr. Ragoczy. There was a similar sickness five years ago that caused a couple of fatalities. Perhaps you remember." I saw his eyebrow raise just slightly when I mentioned deaths in the plural: the public could have only known of Matthew's.

"I'm afraid I don't," he said. "But by all means, continue."

"A young boy died, as did an important man, Mr. Gaines

of Sero Electric. I think you likely remember his death, as you have such significant stock in the company that his brother now runs. The change in leadership must have been memorable, if nothing else." I studied his impassive face. "You also have significant holdings in Achman's Orchards, which ships a regular supply of arsenic to Sero Electric, the company that has accused Panrose of polluting the water supply, and the company that stands to gain if Panrose falls." I resisted leaning in for the kill, instead pinning him with my eyes. "The water flowing from the pipes of the Hill is laced with arsenic." Felicity looked stunned that I'd laid almost all our cards out, but I saw the tiniest flame of respect in Ragoczy's eyes before he quenched it with hard, cold ice.

"And your point is?"

"What's the truth about this odd string of facts, all of which connect rather pointedly to you?"

"What's the truth, you ask? Miss Harper, how would you define truth?" Light from an overhead floating lamp winked off his spectacles, creating the eerie illusion for a moment that he had no eyes. Somehow, I knew he was not merely being evasive with his question. Any other suspect would have been, but Ragoczy was truly posing a philosophical question.

"If one defines truth as anything other than simple reality, no words from that person's mouth could ever be trusted."

"Ah," he said slowly, sluggish red liquid traipsing through the tubes into his veins, "but what is trust, really? How can you expect anyone to trust anyone else? All are merely looking out for their own interests."

"Only a self-interested person would say so," I countered, rolling my pen over my palm. "The greatest of all said that we should look out not only for our own interests but for the interests of others. You are only confirming what I suspect of you, Mr. Ragoczy."

"Don't we always confirm what we think of others in our own minds? Who's to say that's not your own truth about me?

Merely what you *want* to believe? Perhaps a person is not simple as you say, but multi-faceted, a reality that is more like a prism than a mirror."

"You are twisting my words."

"Reality is an illusion, just like a prism, Miss Harper. If you say differently, you are deluding yourself."

"Choosing to believe something doesn't make it true; though it certainly makes it easier to be a crook if your conscience has been battered and locked up in a room of prisms." I paused and smoothed my trousers, willing my hands not to shake. "Only truth sets us free."

He regarded me for a moment, and I saw the threat in his countenance. "Truth is a construct, and you have made yourself chief builder. You, of all people, should know that freedom is the truest illusion. Power only belongs to those who know how to make that illusion gleam most brightly."

I shook my head. He settled further back into his chair, and the lamplight reflection on his glasses hid his eyes again. The lines of his face were those of a man who smiled only for irony, never for genuine enjoyment.

"Mr. Ragoczy, are you one of the parties involved in poisoning the residents of Oak Hill with arsenic?"

He looked at me with something like pity in his expression. "I have no earthly idea what you are referring to. Who is your source?"

"Your public records speak clearly enough without the aid of any source. Do you really claim that you are not pulling the strings behind this conspiracy? Not prompting a Dr. Xavier to prescribe arsenic pills to an important man and then poisoning his water to overdose him, while also sending more people to your hospital for profit? Not having that same doctor five years later prescribe an unreasonable amount of Fowler's Solution to a business associate who then has the arsenic necessary to poison another water supply, framing a successful competitor in the process?" I took a deep breath. "You are, perhaps, unaware that the water on the Hill has been poisoned and people are dying because of a petty business battle?"

"You have many theories, Miss Harper, but I considered you a proper journalist before you posed me these questions. You seem to have fallen far." He leaned forward, and I mirrored him in defiance. The steel in his voice was suddenly sharp and deadly. "Real journalists have facts, not wild theories. There are millions of connections across this city, and yet you have latched onto the ones that tie my hard-earned money to this imaginary scheme of yours. You ought to be ashamed of yourself." The lines of his face relaxed into its accustomed smile of irony.

"Mr. Ragoczy — "

"I'm not finished." He stood, and I followed suit, refusing to be cowed. "You have traced a few of my stock holdings to what seems to be a fishy undertaking, yes. But I have many connections of which you know *nothing*." His head was suddenly only two feet from mine, his hands braced on his desk. The tubes strained as he moved, and though he must be ill, there was not a trace of the invalid about his manner. "My money has power you can only dream of. Your only power is in your writing. And writing, Eugenia?" He tapped my notepad with a thick finger and dropped his voice. "That can be taken from you. Look at yourself. You are merely a vulgar little girl who understands nothing of my world." He let his gaze travel scornfully down my figure and finally graced me with a condescending smile as he eased himself back into his throne. "You want to throw your self-righteous weight around? Go somewhere else. I cannot be intimidated by a reporter from the *Franklin Journal*."

I stood staring at him, willing my fury to subside, unable to summon a single word in response.

"That's a lovely painting," Felicity said suddenly, swinging her feet and propping her chin on her hand. Ragoczy and I swiveled our eyes to her in shock. We'd forgotten her presence. "Behind you." She waved to an oil painting of an old mansion. Ragoczy turned to it slowly as she continued. "I find it bewitching — just the bees' knees. Did you paint it?"

His expression was one of contempt. "Do I *look* like a painter, Miss Jacks?"

"Ah," said Felicity with relish, "but looks can be deceiving, wouldn't you agree? Especially when it comes to women writers." She turned to me briskly. "If you're done, Miss Harper, I'm awfully bored." She wrinkled her nose in a cheeky grin, and quick as a viper, brought her camera up and snapped a photo of the controlled rage of our philosophical host. "I think Mr. Ragoczy could use some time to figure out how to keep the law from grabbing him by his fat ankles." She popped out of her chair and sashayed toward the door, her camera dangling from her hand. I stood and followed its hypnotic swing as if in a trance.

Just before I was out of sight, I glanced back at Ragoczy's livid face. "The truth will come out — whether I write it or not."

For the life of me, I could think of nothing else to say, so when he opened his mouth, I simply left, closing the door on whatever words he had chosen.

12

For once, Felicity and I were silent as we walked. It was as if we had just undergone a trial by fire together, and a bond between us had been forged when she spoke up for me.

"Thank you," I said finally, after a couple of blocks. I stuffed my hands into the pockets of my trousers.

She cocked her head and twinkled at me. "Do I get to hear all of your secrets now?"

"What?" I tripped over a crack in the sidewalk and yanked my hands back out of my pockets. "What are you talking about?"

"Oh," she said airily. "I thought we were having a special moment." She paused for a split second. "You're welcome."

"You know," I said, smiling lopsidedly, "If you end up selling my scoops to your friend at the *Blue Rose* like my last assistant, I'll forgive you. Standing up to Ragoczy earns you a pass in my book."

She made a mock, scandalized sound. "Selling your scoops! What kind of fiend would do that?"

"Well, it happened. And I wouldn't blame you for doing the same. You knew Will long before you met me... plus, the

Blue Rose pays a good rate, and the *Franklin* can't really compete."

"Oh, honey." She glanced at me pityingly, her eyes wicked. "You gotta know. I always get what I want — without giving up anything. I like this job. I'm not going to throw away these good times for a little hard cash. And let me tell you, Felicity Jacks is no snitch." She tossed her head and gave me a smile. "I knew the minute I met you, I wouldn't be playing you for anything. You're that kind of quality."

I was touched. "I... thank you." A reluctant laugh escaped me. "And truly, I mean what I said about Ragoczy. Thank you for standing up to him at the end. I didn't know what to say after..."

"After he basically threatened your life? Oh yes. I remember that part, too." She sent a rock flying with the toe of her Mary Janes. "What a piece of work." It was odd to see such a dark look on her usually mischievous face.

I smiled and shook my head. "It's not the first time I've been threatened, and it won't be the last, but I appreciate you caring. It's good that you got to see what it's like to interview a..." I struggled to find the right word.

"A lunatic. He's crazy." She stopped and turned to face me. "Completely crazy." Abruptly, she started walking again. "Can your attractive detective friend arrest him for being crazy? I'd like to watch that."

I chuckled and trotted to catch up. "That makes two of us. I'm meeting him at Mel's now; do you want to come?"

"Sorry," she said. "Can't. I've got some photos to develop." She threw me a sideways wink, her cheeks dimpling. "Barnes told me he'd show me the ropes in the darkroom."

"I don't want to know," I said quickly. She laughed.

"I asked him to show me how to develop prints, and he agreed." She held her hands aloft and wiggled her fingers. "It'll be educational; I promise. I'll walk with you to Mel's, though. For your own safety. Russian brutes can't get past me; never fear."

I choked back another laugh as she flexed her muscles. "Thank you. It's good to know that I have a bodyguard when I need one."

There went that salute again. If she hadn't just stood down a bear in its den for me, I might have scolded her for her ridiculous gesture. As it was… well, it didn't bother me that much.

When she left me at Mel's, I took a moment to order my mind before finding Ward at our usual table. As always, he was tucked into the corner booth diagonal from the front door where he could see everyone coming in and going out. He caught my eye immediately and rose to let me choose my seat. I sat across from him on the squishiest part of the seat, as I always did, where I could see the clock over the swinging kitchen doors.

"What happened?"

In all the time I've known him, Ward has never been one for small talk. I appreciate that about him, truth be told.

"Behold the work of a seasoned journalist." Taking out the sheet of paper that outlined my carefully planned interview, I waved it at him, then crumpled it and leaned back against the red cushioned booth with a sigh. "I failed, Ward." I rubbed my eyes, feeling a headache approaching. "He steered me into a philosophical discussion and then showed me the door. I got absolutely nothing from him."

He narrowed his eyes and smoothed out my paper of questions. "A philosophical discussion? What about?"

"How truth is a construct and reality is a prism, and I'm a self-righteous woman who has no evidence against him, just 'wild theories.'"

Ward's lips twitched. "Oh? So you got to him, did you?"

I opened my eyes and looked at him skeptically. "I really don't think so."

A sunny waitress with red lipstick approached, smiled at our familiar faces, and took our usual orders. As she departed to the kitchen, Ward added a quick dunk of cream to his coffee.

"If he's steering you away from straightforward questioning into philosophy and then claiming you have 'wild theories,' he's guilty," he said.

I smiled grudgingly and leaned back against the worn cushioning. "Since when do you jump to conclusions?"

He raised an eyebrow. "Tell me everything he said, and I wager that I'll have the same opinion at the end. Redirection and stalling are time-honored tactics of guilty people. Now we just have to find out if I'm right." He stirred his coffee and took a sip. "Go ahead, then."

Somehow encouraged, I recounted the conversation as best I could, tapping my fingers on my blank notepad as I talked. He asked clarifying questions as I spoke, and we both stopped when the waitress brought our food.

At the end of my story, Ward was frowning in thought while I chewed my pie without tasting it.

"Do you still think we can convict him?" I asked, dabbing my mouth with a napkin.

"Eventually, yes. But what I'm concerned about now is the Jacobses. You didn't mention their names, did you?"

"Absolutely not," I said, offended. "I'm not new to this job, Ward. I protect my sources."

He appeared lost in thought. "Of course you do. But we think someone — likely Ragoczy — is spying on them, and they pointed us to Ragoczy. If he knows you talked to them, and if they have hard evidence against him — and he knows they have it — they could be in danger." He finished his mashed potatoes and pushed his plate aside, typing something on his oversized morsie. The diner was quiet around us as the lunch crowd was long gone. I found myself staring at a nondescript man in a suit by the window who had come in after me and had been drinking coffee the whole time. He had no briefcase, and he sat as if waiting, now and then stroking the green-striped band on his fedora. His form was too still for my liking. He hadn't once looked over as I'd stared at him.

Ward shifted, and I tore my eyes away from the stranger.

"I find him interesting, too," he said in an undertone. "Want to make a quick visit before you go back to work?"

"The Jacobses?" I murmured. He nodded and stood, putting his hat on with one hand and helping me out of the booth with the other. I counted out some coins on the table and waved to our waitress after we paid at the register.

Glancing at the stranger as we exited, I found him watching us out of the corner of his eye. His gaze quickly slid away from mine.

He was tapping on a morsie as we passed by the window outside.

"I'll keep an eye out," Ward muttered to me. "Just act normally." He took my arm and led me towards the *Journal*, away from the Jacobses' home. After a couple blocks, we stopped at the butcher's, then strolled down a different street, and finally, after he was satisfied that we were not followed, we headed west.

"What are you going to tell them?" I asked. "If someone is listening, how do we get the evidence and still protect them?"

"I sent Arthur a message," he said under his breath. "He's expecting us and will meet us at his home. Rosalie is there now. If he has anything to help us, he'll hand it over now. He said that they'll leave town to stay with his brother until this is resolved."

I felt my hands trembling, partially with the anticipation of taking down the poisoner and partially out of fear for Arthur and Rosalie. "Do you think that's necessary?"

He was quiet for a long moment. I sneaked a look at his face as we walked. "You do, don't you? You think this man might actually cause them harm." I shoved my hands into my pockets and shook my head. "We don't even know for sure that it's Ragoczy — so why am I so afraid of him?"

Ever since I'd left the hospital, it was as if a sort of doom was hanging over me, a feeling of dread that was growing by the moment. I desperately wanted to catch the culprit and end this story, especially for Chastity and Edwin. The atmosphere in Ragoczy's office had infected me somehow. I hated to think that he had gotten under my skin with his veiled threats, but there was something else wrong, too, and I couldn't put my finger on it.

Ward finally spoke. "It's rare to find a person with influence in so many businesses and with the presence of mind to argue with a reporter who knows as much as you do. Most will show discomfort, perhaps even confess, or at least try to escape the situation. Ragoczy stayed cool and threatening. That's a man that I want to watch and a man that I would not care to underestimate. If Arthur feels it would be prudent to leave town, I wish him godspeed."

Unconsciously, I began to hurry. "I wish this were over," I said quietly. "It's been interesting, but I'm ready for the poisoner to be in prison."

"That makes two of us. Have you seen Diggory lately?"

"Not much," I said. "Felicity and I met up with him about a week ago, and I haven't seen him since. I've been worried about him. Why?"

"I saw Rufus playing with one of Feltz's knockers a few days ago." He looked sideways at me with a reluctant half grin. "And I saw Diggory's feet under the market stall nearby."

I sighed. "He didn't want you to see him with a Feltz man." I looked up at the sky in supplication. "Of all things…"

Ward shrugged. "He certainly knows where the tide is turning; I'll give him that. It won't be long before Feltz is the only boss in town. He's taking the others out one by one, and we can't prove a single hit. Corelli is next, and he knows it.

He's holed up on a family estate somewhere, and his gang is going ballistic."

I balled my fists, then relaxed them slowly. "We do what we can, and nothing more is required."

"That's right. And I know you forget this sometimes, but your job is only to tell the story. It's *my* job to get enough information to arrest the criminal, and I'm beholden to you for going above and beyond in this case." He looked over at me with a sympathetic tilt to his mouth, seeing that his words had failed to put me at ease. "Everyone dies eventually. That fact is of inestimable comfort to me sometimes."

I snorted. "Because you will die and be rid of the mess? Or because the evil ones die and get what they're due?"

He chuckled. "Both."

I shook my head.

We were approaching the Jacobses' house now. The feeling of anxiety crept over me again, and I hoped that we'd get the evidence quickly and leave so that they could disappear — just in case. Then perhaps this eerie feeling would go away and I could concentrate on helping Ward get every detail necessary to put away the insidious Samuel Ragoczy.

Ward let me ascend the steps first, and I rang the bell, fidgeting slightly with my notepad. When no one answered, I frowned and looked at Ward, who was eying the door. He stepped forward, and I moved aside as he twisted the handle. It was unlocked.

I expected him to call out, but instead he moved silently inside, his Stunner ready. I followed without thinking and immediately heard the sounds that caused Ward to break into a run toward the back of the house: a scuffling and a muffled cry.

13

Tea was laid out in the parlor. My eyes noted the four china cups in clear detail. I remember even now the pink roses that adorned the white sugar bowl and the gold edging around the saucers. I smelled strawberry shortcake and mint. The teapot was shattered, and pieces of it littered the floor, trailing straight back toward the kitchen — as if something had been dragged through the pieces, scattering them along its path. I saw Ward running — in my mind he moved in slow motion — and then finally, my body reacted to the adrenaline pumping through it, and I, too, ran, thankfully having the forethought to stoop and whip my knife out of my boot.

There was a sunroom at the back of the house after the kitchen. A small table had crashed onto its side, and beyond it, Rosalie was sprawled across a couch.

A woman dressed all in black held a syringe up to Rosalie's arm.

Ward knocked it out of her hand before it pierced Rosalie's skin and hauled her away as I rushed to Rosalie's side.

"Are you hurt?" I asked breathlessly, clutching my knife

just in case and gently checking her arm with my other hand. She didn't respond. Her skin was unmarked, but as I scanned her body, I saw a lump swelling rapidly on her head. She must have been knocked out. I saw the lamp lying on the floor nearby and filled in the blanks. Expecting Ward to have the assassin in custody, I was surprised to find her almost upon me with Ward doubled up behind her.

I saw a flash of glass and metal — the syringe! — and rolled off the couch to the side, kicking the assassin sharply in the stomach, and then shrieking in recognition as I saw her face. Ward was on her immediately, his breath coming in little gasps as he tried to pin her down. I rushed to his aid and wrenched the syringe from her, throwing it out the window in a moment of sheer hysteria. Somehow she slid from Ward's grasp, lithe as a snake, and jabbed at me with a knife — my knife. I screamed and dodged the stolen blade aimed at my heart, grabbing at her hand and pushing it aside, which earned me a reprieve, but only just. The knife traitorously slid across my upper arm and shoulder, slicing a white-hot line through my flesh. I scrambled away and looked back in time to see Ward aiming his Stunner at her. Time slowed as she raised her knife again —

It couldn't have been real, but at the time, clear as day, I saw Gene instead, a glove stretched out instead of a knife, electricity crackling between the fingers. Terror seized my entire body in an iron grip.

Then electricity zapped in an arc across her back. My body shook uncontrollably. I couldn't move or think. But after a few seconds, she still lay prone, and I told myself it was over.

Collapsing against the wall, trying desperately to breathe normally, I hyperventilated. In my mind's eye, the scene before me faded and Nathaniel's blood puddled across a marble floor. Then a dark figure sprawled on the pavement far below me in the evening light replaced Nathaniel. After that, a dancer's body replaced him: her limbs akimbo, her face erased with black scorch marks. Then another woman with a blasted face took her place. And another. The terrors of my past overwhelmed me, and my body shuddered violently.

Ward's face swam into view; I was sitting on the floor, clutching my head in my hands.

"Are you hurt?" He said. I couldn't answer that yet; I had to know something else.

"Is… she… dead?" My breath came in gasps.

"Stunned, unconscious. I handcuffed her to the couch; she will not attack you again. Are you hurt?"

"I… don't… know…" The room was blurring; I didn't know if it was my mind leaving or the sudden tears fogging my vision.

"I… I'm…"

"You're safe, Ginnie. If anyone else were here, they'd have come by now." Ward took off his suit coat and wrapped it around me. My head felt like it was underwater. I tried to fight for sanity, but lost. Ward's eyes darted around the room. "Rosalie. Is she alive?"

"Y-y-yes… knocked… out…"

He found the gash on my shoulder and pressed his handkerchief to it. "Your wound is shallow. You're going to be fine. Breathe with me now. In… out. In… out."

I desperately tried to force air into my spasming lungs, to breathe with him, but I could barely see him through the haze of panic. She had tried to kill me. She had tried to kill him. My eyes widened as my breathing turned even more rapid and shallow. I couldn't seem to stop or to regain control.

Ward took my hand and placed it over the handkerchief; I held it without thinking. Then he took my face in both his hands and breathed slowly and gustily, holding my eyes with his so that I would concentrate with him. Slowly, within a minute, my lungs began expanding in time with his.

My vision cleared completely to see him searching my face with a knit brow. "Better now?"

"Yes." My limbs shook. He let go of my face and laid a hand on my arm.

"Can you stand? Or shall I carry you to another room? We need to figure out what happened here and make sure Arthur is safe."

I nodded, trying to focus on his words, on what we needed to do. When my legs wouldn't support my weight right away, he gingerly wrapped his arms around me and picked me up. I stiffened, heavy with embarrassment, as we lurched across the sunroom. As we passed the assassin, I shuddered and involuntarily buried my face in his shoulder, weak and humiliated. His grip tightened slightly, and his familiar cedar scent mixed with aftershave cut through my fear, calming me enough to relax my limbs as he carried me through the kitchen and back into the parlor. I knew I was blushing furiously as he set me down on the couch, but he acted as if he didn't notice.

"I need to contact Arthur and send for help," he said. "I'm concerned about Rosalie."

I took a deep breath and let it out slowly, lying with my feet propped on the armrest, concentrating on his voice. "If you can move her in here, I will examine her again while you send your messages. I… can't go back in there."

He nodded. "There is nothing wrong with you," he said. "What you're experiencing is a normal reaction. Keep breathing and focus on what needs to be done."

He tapped a quick message on his morsie and went back to retrieve Rosalie just as the door opened and Arthur appeared in the doorway. His eyes found me immediately and widened in alarm.

"What's wrong?"

"Arthur?" Ward reappeared, holding Rosalie. Arthur gave a shout and leapt forward.

"What's wrong with her?"

"She was attacked. I've sent for help. Her attacker is in the sunroom, immobilized and unconscious. Others will be here soon to take her to the station."

I quickly scooted to the side of the couch. Ward handed Rosalie to Arthur, who gently set her next to me.

"Her? Her attacker was a woman?" Arthur felt Rosalie's forehead.

"Ragoczy's secretary," I croaked. "His nurse. That's who it is."

Arthur's face blanched, and Ward took out his morsie again.

"That was her? You're sure?"

"Yes," I nodded.

Arthur was running his hands over his wife, checking her pulse and scanning for other wounds. He seemed satisfied that she was merely unconscious from the blow to her head and otherwise uninjured.

"I'm going to check the house to make sure there are no more surprises," Ward said. "Then I will need to leave."

"You're going after Ragoczy?" I asked.

"Yes."

"Take me with you — please." I rolled over and stood to show that I was fit. The floor spun a bit, but I blinked and pressed the handkerchief to my shoulder. "I'll make a better bandage and be ready when you are."

He paused, thinking, and it was then that I noticed the crimson liquid staining his midsection.

"Ward! What —?" I rushed to him, and he glanced down to see what I was looking at.

"Ah," he said. "That explains things."

"Do you want me to look at it?" I asked. "Did she stab you?"

"She certainly tried," he admitted. He unbuttoned his shirt, and Arthur joined us in examining the wound.

"Ragoczy's secretary is his enforcer," Arthur said quietly as he pressed a clean towel to Ward's abdomen. He retrieved a small box from the kitchen and glanced up into the corner of the parlor as he pulled out a needle and thread.

"Do you have enough for two?" Ward asked dryly. He pointed to my shoulder in answer to Arthur's questioning look.

"Oh dear! Please be seated, Miss Harper. I will attend to you next; keep that cloth pressed tightly! As I was saying, his 'secretary' came to us after Matthew died, told us to quiet down about the poisoning… and told us what would happen if we didn't." He worked quickly and efficiently, finishing Ward's stitches and then cleaning the needle before coming to kneel before me. I showed him my shoulder and upper arm, and he grimaced.

"Ah… I can stitch it for you, Miss Harper, but, um, wouldn't you rather have the privacy of the hospital? You see…" He colored. "You'd have to remove your blouse."

I flushed, and Ward coughed and moved into the kitchen — presumably to begin his house search. My modesty fought with my desire to confront Ragoczy in person. "Do you… er… have a sheet I could use, perhaps?" I asked, feeling brazen.

"Of course," Arthur said. "And I could get you one of Rosalie's shirts." He ran down the hallway as I removed Ward's coat from my shoulders and unbuttoned my blouse. Holding the coat in front of me, I took the sheet from Arthur, who averted his eyes as I wrapped my upper half in the sheet, leaving my left shoulder bare. My face hot with embarrassment, I bit my lip as he cleaned the wound and placed a cream on it that dulled the pain before he inserted the needle.

"What happened after she threatened you?" Ward called from the sunroom.

"They gave me a choice: move here, to the west side, and go to work for Ragoczy at the hospital where he could monitor me and use my knowledge of blood transfusions, or they would kill Rosalie. They knew about my work with blood transfusions in the war, and somehow they knew that what I'd experimented with was… not exactly legal. Ethical, I would say, but not strictly legal. Matthew had just passed, and we were numb with grief. Rosalie hardly cared if she died, but I knew I couldn't live if she was gone, too. I agreed to their terms. I've been working there since, mostly as Ragoczy's personal doctor. He has a rare blood condition and needs constant transfusions, or his blood will clot and kill him. I've been working on a treatment for his ailment for the past four years." He stopped talking as he finished the stitches and cut the thread. I looked away, feeling nauseous again. "We knew when we moved here that they were spying on us. I found the device immediately. We've been trapped — prisoners in our home — ever since."

"I'm sorry," I whispered.

He opened his mouth to answer, but at that moment, Rosalie stirred.

"Rosie!" He was at her side instantly.

"Arthur?" She winced as she opened her eyes.

A thought came to me as I pulled on the borrowed blouse and buttoned it, then pulled the sheet out from under the blouse. I peered into the corner over the bookcase. "Aren't they listening now?"

Rosalie sighed.

"I broke it when you told me that Detective Ward was coming. That's why she came to kill me, isn't it?"

"Unlikely," Ward said, suddenly appearing beside me from the hallway. "Ragoczy made a mistake. Miss Harper must have spooked him with her questions today, and he decided to act rather than wait for us to get the evidence from you." He gave Arthur a hard look. "You do have evidence, don't you? I'll need it for the warrant."

"It's here," Arthur said. He stood and walked to the hallway, flicked on the light, and crept his fingers along the wall until a plate depressed and then opened, revealing a small safe, which he unlocked. He pulled several papers from it as well as a vial with clear liquid inside. "These are the papers proving that the water was laced with arsenic. These," he handed Ward an envelope, "are photos of Ragoczy's men pouring it into the well. This is a sample of the water itself. I hope it's enough. I spent a year gathering it all, but it wasn't enough then. Confronting him did no good: Matthew had just died. And he'd already bribed the newspapers to keep silent when I went to them. And then… I had Rosalie to think of. If he'd killed her because I went to the police… but I'm still sorry I didn't bring it to you sooner." He looked very old as he handed the vial to Ward, and I wondered if guilt kept him up at night: guilt that he hadn't found enough in time to save his son. I put a hand on Rosalie's arm, and she smiled sadly at me.

"It's time for him to see justice," she whispered, her bruised face fierce.

I squeezed her arm gently and stood.

"We'll need the warrant first?"

Ward nodded and opened the door for me. Three policemen and a nurse stood poised just outside. One man had a beefy hand outstretched to knock.

"Impeccable timing," Ward said and motioned them inside. "We'll leave you to it. The perpetrator is in the back sunroom, cuffed to the couch. I checked her a moment ago and she was still unconscious. Use extreme caution with her, especially if she awakens."

Their faces grew grim as they took in his blood-stained shirt.

"Miss Harper, if you're ready, let's be off."

14

"If you have to get a warrant, won't it take too long for us to arrest Ragoczy today?" I trotted to keep up with Ward's long strides.

"I have a shortcut," he said. "Are you tired?" He slowed, but I gestured him on.

"I want to get this done as quickly as you do. I can keep up."

A few blocks passed in our silence. Shame grew inside me. At last, I had to say something.

"Ward..." I swallowed. "I'm sorry for panicking. I was useless... I don't know what happened. I saw something that wasn't... wasn't... real..."

I broke off, biting my lip.

Ward gave me a keen look and hesitated before speaking. "After my first skirmish in France, I saw the faces of men I'd bayonetted for years afterward. I still do, sometimes. Mostly in dreams."

I shuddered and glanced over at him. He was peering steadily at the road ahead.

"I don't know why, but fear can bring back that experience just as if it is happening again. Most of my comrades suffered the same way. It's not your fault you saw something and panicked when she attacked you. You've faced death before. It's bound to leave a mark."

"How do you stay so cool in conflict?" I asked despairingly. "You've seen far worse things than I."

He shrugged. "Use what I've told you. Remember where you are. Breathe deeply. Relax your body. It can get better over time. I don't suffer now the way I did before." He eyed me. "Are you still writing about your cases?"

"Yes," I said, feeling silly.

"Does it help?"

"I think so."

"Then continue the habit. And…" He directed me around a gaggle of elderly women who were too excited to pay attention to where they were going. "Don't be embarrassed. You have more courage than most people I know. This doesn't erase that fact."

"What are you talking about?" My voice cracked. "I'm a coward. And not just then." I threw my hand behind me. "I'm afraid all the time."

He stopped at the edge of the curb. I stopped, too, watching traffic lurch by with hollow eyes. When he turned to me, I met his eyes reluctantly.

"There's a difference between courage and foolhardiness," he said. "I've seen you run from things a fool would not, and I've seen you run *to* things a coward would not. You don't lack courage simply because you're afraid — the important thing is where and when you run."

A reprieve in traffic broke his gaze from mine. He held out his arm, and I took it as we crossed the street.

I had nothing to say to respond to his kind words, but one of his gifts was companionable silence. With an effort, I let myself settle into that silence while I worked to keep up with his decisive march toward the harbor.

"Where are we going, exactly?" I asked when I realized the courthouse was not our destination.

"Arnold Devons' house," Ward said. "He's a judge and sits on the bench on weekends. He's an odd character, but when I need a warrant quickly, he's my source."

"I've covered some Saturday hearings," I said. "They're rather... well, like a circus sometimes."

"He'd make an excellent ringleader." Ward cracked a rare grin. "This is his house."

We faced a brick row house with a forest green door and a pot of cheerful pansies beside it. I was pleased with the effect.

"How does his wife deal with his antics?"

"He doesn't have one. He lives alone." Ward let me ascend first and then rapped on the handsome door.

A man in a smart pin-striped suit opened the door almost immediately and brightened at the sight of Ward.

"Tommy! It's been too long! Not very many interesting cases lately, eh? Come in, come in, and introduce me to your friend."

The door closed silently behind us as we stepped into a beautiful parlor with pure white furniture and a yellow rug. My shoulders instantly relaxed in the calming lavender-scented atmosphere. Floating lights twinkled merrily with a soft glow, and fine art decorated the walls. Though it had been some time since I'd made the rounds of art exhibits with my wealthy family, I recognized the style of several famous artists. One small piece in the corner over an oak credenza caught my eye in particular.

"Is that a Brandtley?" I blurted, momentarily forgetting both the trauma of the afternoon *and* my manners. I put one hand over my mouth and offered the other to the beaming man. "So sorry. I'm Ginnie, Ginnie Harper. You have a lovely home."

"Miss Harper," he said with relish, shaking my hand with both of his. A faint hint of cologne wafted over me.

"Marvelous to meet you." He looked quizzically at Ward out of the corner of his eye as he asked me, "Haven't I seen your name in the paper, dear? The *Franklin* perhaps?"

"Yes, I'm a reporter," I said. "I'm investigating the poisoner of Oak Hill, which is why I've come with Detective Ward."

His face relaxed into a broad smile, and he shot Ward a wink. "Ah, I see what has brought you to my doorstep! A famous story, no less! You're in the climax of your case, I assume, Tommy? Need a warrant post-haste?"

Ward nodded. "For Mr. Samuel Ragoczy. I have the evidence right here. He's behind the poisoning of the Hill — with arsenic — and is also linked to a case about five years ago on the north side for the same thing: arsenic poisoning of a water supply. That poisoning may have directly or indirectly caused the death of a Mr. Benjamin Gaines. Miss Harper has more information for the current crime, along with my notes here, and these papers are for the previous poisoning."

I took out my notes and handed them over as Ward did, feeling anxious. My fears were unfounded, however.

"Tommy, Tommy," he chuckled as he leafed through the papers. "My utter trust in your gut instinct has never failed us yet. This is quite enough for me to go on, but I'm trusting you to connect the dots so we don't get any unnecessary reproofs." He shuffled the papers and handed them back. "Do sit down. I'll be back momentarily." As he headed down the hall, he called back, "Yes, Miss Harper, it is a Brandtley. *Arnold* Brandtley — that's me."

I turned to Ward in bemusement as he disappeared. "Does he mean he *is* Brandtley, the artist? Or that he is related to him?"

Ward shrugged. "His name is Arnold B. Devons; that much I know. What he does in his spare time, I have no idea, though now that you mention it, he does seem to have a rather… artistic sense." He looked around the room doubtfully. I laughed in disbelief.

"Brandtley is a recluse! He sends his paintings to art shows via proxy and never attends in person! I've always loved his work. There's something…" I stood and crossed the room, peering at the painting in the corner. "captivating about it. The way he uses light. It's unique."

Ward joined me and frowned at the painting. "It's certainly pretty," he offered, and I snorted.

"You'd make very fine company at an art show." I leaned in more closely to the painting. "I think that's the view of the harbor from the end of this street."

Judge Devons reappeared, papers in hand. "Here's your warrant, old fellow," he said. "Use it well. And Miss Harper, do put me in your article, won't you now? As a judge," he added hastily. "I keep Arnold Brandtley under wraps. No publicity. That's why I use my middle name only."

"Did you paint this?" I asked, dying to know for sure.

"I did." He winced. "It's absurd, but my housekeeper found it in the attic and put it there. It doesn't go with all *these*." He gestured broadly around the room's paintings with a proud look. "I'm fortunate to have some real masterpieces here." He sent a frown into the corner and spoke confidingly. "I must take it down; it's just that she absolutely terrifies me. British. Commanding manner. Utterly undeniable, you know."

I grinned again. "I know the type. My housekeeper was the same. I think you ought to keep it up, though. It's a lovely rendering of the docks at dawn. I find it enchanting."

"Do you now?" He lit up like one of his twinkling lamps. "Well." His chest expanded, and he clapped Ward on the back. "I'm sure you're in a hurry, so I won't keep you. But you must both come back for supper some time, you hear? I won't take no for an answer. And Tommy boy," he gave Ward a chiding glance as we walked out to the front stoop. "None of that army spy business this time. I won't have it coming back on me again."

Ward frowned at him with the barest hint of chagrin. "That was fifteen years ago, Brandtley. For heaven's sake, forget it."

Brandtley chortled. "I refuse to forget it. Especially not when you bring pretty reporters around. Well, go on then. Arrest that poisoner. I'd love a signed copy of the *Franklin*, Miss Harper. If you don't mind." He winked and closed the door on my astonished face.

"Something else, isn't he?" Ward said dryly as we turned to the street.

"I think I've run into more interesting characters this week than I have in the last three years," I said truthfully.

Ward raised his eyebrows at me and flagged a cab. "You need to come around with me more."

Glancing around us, I spotted a man in a fedora standing by the lamppost down by the docks reading a newspaper. He had just stepped into view as Ward entered the cab. I squinted at his fedora, but he walked away before I could determine its color. Feeling paranoid, I stepped into the cab, thankful to rest my feet while we sped to West Hospital.

The ride was quiet, which helped me compose my mind for what we were about to do. I had been nicely distracted from our mission with the pleasure and shock of meeting my favorite artist, but now my mind was preoccupied again with Ragoczy. How would he react? Would he become violent? One never knew about these sorts of men. Though they seemed refined and above forceful outbursts, sometimes the most rich and respected became animalistic when their way of life was threatened. I had seen such things happen before, and when I called to mind his cold eyes, I did not doubt that Ragoczy was one of those men. Trying to hold off the terrors of the past two hours, I spent the cab ride deciding how to respond if he did indeed resort to force.

Ward noted me tapping out an invisible sonata on the top of my thighs, and, when we alighted in front of the hospital and he helped me out of the cab, he gave my hand a light squeeze.

When I looked at him in surprise, his eyes glinted in a way that reminded me of other times he'd made arrests.

"Ready to see justice?" he asked.

"I don't think you are supposed to *enjoy* arresting someone," I said with a reluctant smile. "But I must admit, I am looking forward to it."

"Thank you for doing all the hard work for me," he said as we trotted up the path to the hospital entrance. "It's rare that I get to arrest someone after sitting on my hands all week."

"You were hardly sitting on your hands," I retorted. "Giving me the Jacobses as contacts and investigating Ragoczy's records… We had an entire team working on this one. Felicity was really —" I gasped. "I forgot to tell Felicity anything that happened this afternoon! She'll be so disappointed to be left out." I grimaced. "I guess I'm just not used to having a real assistant again."

"Well, we're not waiting for her," Ward said practically. "We're here."

We walked past the empty secretary desk and opened Ragoczy's office door without knocking.

"Samuel Ragoczy?" Ward said with authority. "I'm Detective Ward, and —"

His morsie pinged as I collapsed onto a chair, exhaling in shock. It seemed I hadn't had my fill of death yet today.

15

Ragoczy was curled on the floor in a fetal position. Mottled and pale, he appeared to have been focusing on something just before he died; his eyes were wide open, and his face was contorted in a grimace, or perhaps a growl. His transfusion machine was on its side; it seemed to have crashed to the ground with him. Red leaked onto the carpet, staining it a dead brown.

Horror rose in me with the bile that filled my throat.

"How…?" I choked.

Ward was examining the body, frowning in concentration. "Yes. How did a murderer slip in and out of here in the middle of the day — at a busy hospital?"

"Are you sure… he was murdered… he certainly looks it, but…" I shuddered. "Perhaps he… fell?" It sounded inane, even to me. There was something wrong, something in his face, that told me otherwise.

"The timing is too convenient, and look here: bruising on the arms and skin under the fingernails of this hand. I'm open to the possibility that it was an accident, but I will be surprised if it's true." He picked up his morsie and scanned the message that printed. His frown deepened. "She's escaped."

"What? Porter has?"

"They went to the sunroom, and she was gone. She left the handcuffs."

I refused to panic again. Concentrating on the rise and fall of my chest, I tried to work through the problem logically. "So he sent her to kill the Jacobses, and meanwhile someone came here to kill him. Then she escaped. Did she kill him? Was he *not* the one behind this scheme after all?" The questions spun in my head, but I found that holding them there and examining them helped my breathing stay even and my heartbeat steady. No visions rose to torture me.

Ward laid aside his morsie and the warrant and pulled on gloves. "Stay where you are, if you please, Miss Harper. The coroner will be here soon. I'm going to search the room and start the murder investigation. I just notified police across the city to search for the secretary. Her name is Emmeline Porter — though perhaps that is an alias." He stopped. "Actually, if you are well enough, would you be willing to take your autophone and interview the people in the building? There shouldn't be many people left in the office, and I'd like to catch them before they leave. Please tell them no one should leave until we give the word."

I got to my feet, feeling the exhaustion of the day creeping up on me. But there was more to this story that I had not uncovered yet, and determination overcame my tiredness.

"Yes," I said. "Is there anything else I can do?"

Ward shook his head, focused on examining Ragoczy's desk. On my way to the door, my eyes caught the barest flash of black, like someone's hat, in the window. Startled more than I should have been, I scanned the sidewalk outside but saw nothing. I shook my head. It was probably a bird. Was paranoia simply a natural outcome of coming too close to being a murder victim?

Rounding up the hospital office employees turned out to be an easy enough task, and getting word to the rest of the hospital that no one was to leave was simpler than I expected. The hospital had a superior communication system, which made sense when I considered all that needed to be communicated in a medical facility.

What was baffling was that no one — no one — had seen anyone enter or exit Ragoczy's office, even though it was central to this part of the building and in plain view of every other office.

"And you neither heard nor saw anything out of place in the last few hours? No one coming in or out of the office? No one outside?" I repeated the same questions to every person and grew more and more convinced that the murderer was either a professional the likes of which I had never seen, or the killer was a ghost. Curiosity drove me to the waiting rooms, the staff rooms, the hallways, but no one had seen anything out of place, or anyone other than the normal staff and patients. I investigated the windows outside (thinking again of the black flash I had seen) and all the entrances that could lead to the office, looking over my shoulders as I did in case Miss Porter had returned. Ragoczy's office was entirely closed off in this section of the hospital and only accessible (as far as I could tell) by a single locked window that faced the street and by his windowed office door.

Bafflement was an inadequate word to describe what I was feeling as I made my way back to Ward, who was now standing at the side of the room, leafing through a thick, black book.

Wearily, I handed him the autophone.

"I doubt you'll find anything helpful on there. Have you discovered anything?" My interest peaked when I saw his intent expression. "What is it?"

Without looking up, he said, "You were right about all of it; I congratulate you. Dr. Xavier is on Ragoczy's payroll, and Mrs. Benjamin Gaines sends a fee every year to him — likely for the murder of her husband and for keeping quiet about it.

Every trail is marked here. Our victim was an extensive records keeper. We'll be searching his home as well, but…" he shrugged, "unless he kept duplicates, he seemed to have thought his office to be safer than his home for important papers. I found his safe with years of records in it — as well as a wireless receiver that probably matches the audi-spy in the Jacobses' house."

My eyes lit up. "How did you open the safe? Did you find the combination somewhere?"

He finally glanced up and met my eyes with an odd expression. "It wasn't locked."

My lips parted as my jaw went slack.

Ward studied me for a moment, but I had the idea that his mind was far away. "I could be wrong, but I believe the murderer cracked the safe and left it open — for us."

"But why?" I asked. My brows contracted. A crime of vengeance? Perhaps someone knew that he was the poisoner and came after him? Did Miss Porter turn on her employer after her attempt on the Jacobses — perhaps out of fear for failing him? My stomach dropped as I considered another option. "The murderer couldn't have been Arthur, could it have, Ward? Surely he wouldn't have been so foolish!"

"Naturally, we'll look into him," he said with a knit brow. "But I don't believe so, no. If he was in his department all afternoon, that will be easy to prove. He works with several people on the other side of the hospital."

The coroner had arrived while I was interviewing people and now strode over to us, removing his gloves. His thick camera bounced on his chest as he walked. Several policemen stood in the receiving area outside; their murmurs were like the undercurrent of a river that was rushing by too quickly for me to keep up. Had I really only met Ragoczy this afternoon? Only found out this morning that it was arsenic that he was dumping in the water through Gaines? My head spun, and I put up a hand to rub my shoulder without thinking. I winced.

The wound was beginning to ache again. The effects of Arthur's medicinal paste must be wearing off.

The coroner was speaking. "I don't know for certain yet, but at this point, it looks as though his death was due to his blood transfusion machine malfunctioning. I see signs of blood clots. You say his nurse was not here this afternoon?"

I shivered involuntarily.

"She would have been gone from about two thirty to four o'clock," Ward said. "We don't know where she has been after that."

"He's been dead since about three o'clock, I believe." He glanced at his watch. "I'll need to do more tests to be certain. But he was seen through the window alive at two forty-five by a coworker, and no one has entered the office since then — until you two."

"A simple malfunction when he was under suspicion in the Hill poisoning seems very unlikely. The timing clears Miss Porter if it was indeed murder, and it ought to clear Arthur, if you confirm that as the time of death," Ward said to me. He paused, frowning at my face, which I can only assume had become rather pale. "Are you well? I think you ought to sit down."

"I'm fine," I said, tapping invisible piano keys on the side of my thigh. "Thank you, though. I'm trying to understand everything that has happened today, and I'm finding it to be beyond me."

Ward lifted an eyebrow. "Naturally. This is a convoluted case. However, your work today is done. I appreciate the interviews you've just completed — and all the research you did that led us to this point. You ought to go home and get some rest. I'll catch you up tomorrow for your article."

His words only frustrated me. "I'll leave this with you then," I said, keeping my composure and leaving the autophone. "Good evening."

Crossing the street to the *Journal*, I finally realized what was wrong with me — besides the fact that I had become so neurotic that I was looking over my shoulder every five paces. No, what was wrong was that I was suffering from acute disappointment. Our main poisoning suspect was dead. The one who should be behind bars for what he'd orchestrated, for the little boy he'd murdered, for my brother-in-law's illness, was dead. He would never stand trial. He'd never help us uncover the others who had a part in these poisonings. We'd have to do that ourselves. Meanwhile, his murderer was at large, and an assassin was wandering the streets after attacking Rosalie, Ward, and me. It was all very unsettling and disturbing — not at all what I had envisioned for the tail end of this case.

My head pounded. My shoulder ached as I pushed open the door to the *Journal*. I rolled my arm back and massaged my neck as I crossed the room.

Ripping the cover off my typewriter, I sat with a thump at my desk, staring unseeingly at the blank roll of paper tucked into the top of the faithful machine.

Rubbing my hand over its shining black surface, I thought of the stories that would likely pile on my desk after this full day. I could almost see the headlines in front of me:

"Sero Electric Bankrupt After Poisoned Water Scandal"

"Panrose Electric's Stock Skyrockets"

"West Hospital Under Scrutiny After Key Leader Poisons Oak Hill Residents"

"Hospital Mogul Found Dead in Office"

"Would-Be Murderer Escapes After Injuring Woman, Reporter, and Detective"

I put my head on my desk and covered it with my hands.

I couldn't do it. The story wasn't finished.

Surely Gaines would be arrested and more compatriots found. Ward would go on the search for Ragoczy's murderer and for Miss Porter.

But right now, with the hum of the newsroom all around

me, I couldn't muster up the courage to write the story of the Oak Hill Poisoner. This morning I had held the unraveling knot in my hands, confident that I was close to making a noose for the poisoner. But now? Now I was holding a burning wick, and for all I knew, it led to a stick of dynamite.

Who had killed Ragoczy?

And why hadn't I been allowed a second chance to stand up to him?

16

When Felicity found me, the red light of sunset was streaming through the windows of the newsroom. She perched herself on the desk corner, watching me banging away at the typewriter.

"How are you?" she asked quietly. I didn't notice the change in her normal tone; instead, I drew my lips together in a pinched line and finished my paragraph with a whack to the cartridge. It sprang across in a satisfied "ping!" and I turned in my chair and looked at her with blurry eyes.

"Ragoczy is dead, and his nurse tried to kill us. Ward —"

"I know," she said, rolling her eyes. "Everyone knows what happened. This is a newspaper. You've had at least two reporters reading over your shoulder throughout the evening and then telling *everyone* about it. I asked how *you are*. Remember that part about someone trying to kill you? Why are you here?"

"Doing my job," I muttered, rubbing my eyes.

"You can't face it, can you?"

"No."

She regarded me thoughtfully for a moment, swinging her legs. "Come on."

"What?" I asked tiredly.

"Did you finish your article?" When I nodded, she ripped the paper from the cartridge and jumped to the floor. "Then come on."

Too weary to protest, I let her lead me to Mac's office, where she deposited the paper and left without so much as a by-your-leave when he opened his mouth to berate me for the lateness of my story.

She pulled me out the door, past the reporters who tried to congratulate us.

"Where are we going?" I managed to ask after I'd freed my hand from her grip. We were walking toward the harbor, and I couldn't for the life of me think why. "Felicity?"

"It's your *surprise*," she said. "Remember? Five o'clock. We're a little late, but better late than never."

"It… slipped my mind," I said, sarcasm coloring my voice. "With everything else going on… almost being murdered…"

"Oh, you're going to hold that over my head forever, aren't you?" she asked. Her bright red lipstick flashed into a smile. "Come on, we're almost there."

The river came into view, and a voice wafted to us from one of the row houses. "Back so soon, Miss Harper?"

I turned to see Judge Devons, or rather, Brandtley, standing on his stoop, watching the sunset with a pipe in his mouth.

I waved.

"Hellooo," Felicity called. "Isn't he an eyeful?" she added in an undertone. I turned to her in astonishment.

"He's at least twice your age, Felicity."

"Mmm. How do you know him?" She was heading straight toward the water.

"I met him this afternoon. He's a judge and an —" I stopped, trying to decide if he would want me to reveal his secret.

"Ooh, a judge with something to hide, is he?" She

sounded delighted. "Let's stop and talk on the way back. We'll be back!" she called out, waving to him.

"Felicity, you realize this road ends in a very wet drop-off, don't you?"

She rolled her eyes and grabbed my hand again. Her purse clunked against my arm, and I wondered again what she carried that made such a racket. "And you realize you're a wet blanket, don't you? We're going on the water, silly!"

"*On* the water?"

She led me out onto one of the docks and busied herself untying the rowboat moored there.

"Is this your boat?"

"No." Her wicked eyes danced at my shocked look. "But it *is* David's, and he told me to use it whenever I feel like it. He's studying abroad right now."

I decided not to ask who David was.

"Hop in. There's something out there that I want to show you."

I accordingly "hopped," and thankfully, the boat was sturdy enough to withstand my awkward movements. I had never been comfortable on the water, though my father had insisted that my siblings and I learn to swim when we were very young. His brother had drowned when they were children. I had had little occasion for swimming since I had left his house, and I hoped I wouldn't find occasion for it tonight.

"Are you sure you know how to row this… vessel?" I asked dubiously, clinging to the sides, wondering why on earth I had let her bring me out here. I should have insisted on going home to bed. My head and shoulder were aching terribly now. "I really ought to go home," I said hopelessly.

She gave me a stern look. "You really ought to sit back and relax. You've just had a horrible ordeal. I'm going to show you something to drive it all from your pretty little head."

I rolled my eyes. "I've seen water before, Felicity."

She sniffed and gave me no satisfaction of an answer.

Adjusting myself on the narrow seat, I sighed and settled back against the bow as Felicity rowed from the middle with the only set of oars. She headed upstream toward the middle of the great river. The other bank was distant during the day, but tonight I couldn't even see its dark shores. The river seemed to stretch all the way to the curve of the world, where it presumably dropped off into infinity.

No one traversed the gentle current after sunset except for a few pleasure cruisers, but they were far from us, and their lights and revelry were muted by the quiet sounds of Felicity's rowing. This time, when I sighed, my chest and arms loosened as the air gently left my lungs. Away from the lights of the city, the stars were free to twinkle majestically against the indigo velvet stretched between the horizons. Another sigh left my chest, and with it, some of the fear and frustration of the day. I hadn't seen stars like this since childhood, and I couldn't look away.

Felicity kept the silence. Her oars made the tiniest of splashes as they exited the water. Glancing down for just a moment, I found myself enraptured by the small eddies they created upon entry. The folds wrinkled the dark depths, and when they stilled, I imagined I could see the reflection of Orion in the water. I cupped my chin and leaned on my knees as tales I had created as a child about his heroic exploits filled my mind. Even now, I could envision his tall, broad form, his Greek nose, and his rippling muscles as he bent his great bow. I smiled to myself as images of my childhood fervor and delight galloped across my mind.

The moon unveiled herself and shone directly onto the water in front of us. I held my breath as we crossed her mystic reflection, my childish fantasy now creating stories of a portal to a magical world of mermaids gliding through reeds and kraken lurking in caves.

I don't know how much time passed before Felicity turned in her seat and we grinned at each other.

"It's wonderful, isn't it?" she whispered, apparently as loath as I to break the spell.

I nodded, not wanting it to end, though my eyelids drooped and my shoulder begged for an aspirin.

"Do you come out here often?"

"You'd think, wouldn't you?" She was silent for a moment, her oars still as we drifted slowly backwards. "I haven't been out here for months, not since just after David went overseas. How is it that we can experience something so… beautiful… and forget the way it makes us feel? Until we really need it again." She smiled at me. "When I saw you this evening, I remembered."

"Thank you."

A knot in my chest had come undone, and though nothing had changed, and the perpetrators of today's horrors still roamed free, peace reigned in my mind, peace in the conviction that all would come right in the end. I thought of Ward's words about finding comfort in the fact that death comes to all, and I almost chuckled.

Felicity cocked her head. "What?"

I didn't get a chance to tell her.

The memory of Ward's words was a little too fitting at that moment.

17

"**G**et down!" I screamed, yanking Felicity into the bottom of the boat. A shot rang out over our heads, and I heard the splash of the bullet ricocheting off the water yards away. Emmeline Porter had emerged from the depths an arm's length away in some sort of metallic gear and had fired a shot at Felicity just as I pulled her down. Shaking, I grabbed an oar and slammed it down toward Porter's head — but she was gone again.

"Are you all right?" I gasped to Felicity, scanning the surrounding water.

"Ye—"

Porter emerged again, several meters away on the other side of the boat. She aimed her gun, saw me watching, and ducked down again, the bullet connecting with the oar that I had reflexively pulled up in front of my chest. The oar slammed against me, and I tipped backwards. Felicity grabbed my vest before I fell into the water. Gripping the sides of the boat to steady myself, I saw the bullet was caught in the last splintered wood layer of the oar. My reflex had probably saved my life. I scanned the black current, shoving Facility back down despite her squeaky protests and holding the oar like the weapon and shield it had become.

Protect her! I screamed to my subconscious as I fought the panic welling up in me. *You can't blank out now! Breathe! Breathe!*

This time I almost hit Porter as she popped up at the stern, where I had clambered, predicting her movement. My oar hit the water where her head had been the moment before.

"Coward!" I didn't know what I was shrieking; all I knew was that fury had overtaken my fear.

"Wait, Ginnie!" Felicity screamed as I swung at the next ripple of water. A hand grabbed the oar and jerked, pulling me in with it.

Hitting the icy water made my entire body clench. Bubbles sprang from my mouth as I yelled in shock. My loose trousers and too-large blouse were weighing me down. I desperately kicked — both to get to the surface *and* to injure my opponent, remembering that Porter must be nearby. My shoe connected with something before I took one hopeful gasp of air and was pulled under again. Opening my eyes did no good; the water was black in the night, but then I glimpsed a flash of metal and reached out for it. I yanked on it with all my might, and a bevy of bubbles blossomed around us. Hoping that I had incapacitated the gear that allowed her to stay underwater, I kicked out for the surface in the opposite direction, stripping my trousers off as I did so. The release of their weight was the last bit of buoyancy I needed, and I breathed more life-giving air before looking around for the boat. To my dismay, it was at least three meters downstream. Just as I struck out for the boat, Porter, propelled by her suit, sprang from the water like a dolphin and vaulted onto the boat, a knife in her hand.

"Felicity!" I screamed, and immediately got a mouthful of water.

I could barely make out what Felicity was doing in the

dark, and what I saw utterly flummoxed me: she appeared to be digging in her purse.

"Hit her with it!" I screamed again, kicking for all I was worth as Porter gained her balance and advanced on Felicity.

Instead of taking my advice, Felicity rose to her feet, legs spread apart for balance, and held out what she'd been hiding in her purse.

The concussive sound of a gun firing jolted across the water, numbing my ears and leaving them ringing. One shot… two… three… four…

Porter jerked and fell into the bottom of the boat just as I reached it.

Her eyes wild, Felicity fired again at the still form.

The sound hit me with more force this time, and I fell back into the water with a splash.

Exhaustion overcame me, and I floated, just trying to keep my head above water.

"Come on, Ginnie! Get in here!" Felicity took hold of my arm, her nails digging into my skin, and hauled me clumsily over the side. "Did she hurt you?" she asked, just as I gasped, "Are you hurt?"

"No," we both said, and with that, we sank into our seats, avoiding the body at the stern.

"We've got to get back," I said, vacantly looking around for the oars. One was in the boat beside me. The other was floating downstream, almost too far away to see.

"Blast," Felicity whispered. Her eyes were enormous; her face was as pale as the moon overhead. "Again."

"Should we go after it?" I asked, looking at the oar in despair.

"I killed her," she said blankly, and then she was weeping into her hands.

"She would have murdered you!" I said, wrapping my arms around her. My wet clothes immediately soaked her jacket. "Oh, I'm sorry!" I rubbed my goose-pimply arms.

"Let's get back to land. Everything will be all right, I promise." My breaths came jerkily as I picked up the oar, aching in every part of my body.

If I could just row us to land, everything would be all right, I told myself. If I could just push the water behind me with the oar... no, harder than that... oh, it was so heavy... and there was a corpse only centimeters from my feet... the water in the boat's bottom was red... and the oar was so heavy...

I looked toward land and saw the silhouette of a man in a fedora walking away. Then the sound of a small motor distracted me, and I turned and stood hastily to see another boat coming our way.

"Miss Harper! Is that you?"

I almost dropped the leaden piece of wood in relief. "Yes! Mr. Brandtley! It's me!" I felt tears running down my face and wiped my eyes to see him better.

"Oh, very good! Your friend — is she all right?"

"Yes, yes, we've just had quite a scare! There's... there's a dead woman in our boat."

"Tried to kill you, eh? Yes, I heard the shots from my porch! Lucky thing I was out tonight! You just hold tight; I'll be right there."

I laid the cursed oar across my lap and fought the urge to lay myself over the top of it. Felicity hugged herself and stared blankly across the water.

Just a few moments passed before he was alongside us, and then he was helping Felicity aboard, with me supporting her back as she clung to him. Once she was seated on his tiny yacht, he unraveled a rope and stepped down to me, hitching our boat to the back of his. We left the body in the rowboat and climbed aboard his larger craft. Thankfully, he asked no questions but simply wrapped Felicity in a blanket that he had stowed in one of the seat compartments, handed me another which I used to cover my exposed legs, and roared the boat back towards the dock.

My morsie was useless, completely waterlogged, but I coaxed Felicity's from her and send Ward a message to meet us at the judge's house. The policeman walking the beat had also heard the shots and was happy to take over Porter's body.

After he had supplied us with hot coffee and brandy, the judge gave me a robe from his guest room to change into, and then endeavored to make us comfortable in his cheery parlor while we waited for Ward. Felicity was doing better; the blanket and coffee had brought some color back into her cheeks, and she was eying Arnold Brandtley Devons with something almost like interest while he distracted me with stories about how he'd procured the art on his walls. I finally stopped shivering, and my hair was warming nicely by the fire when Ward arrived not long after. Having declined brandy and accepted coffee from the judge, he asked us to tell our story. I gave most of the details, though Felicity did pipe up towards the end. When she came to the part where Porter had come at her with a knife, she gave me a pleading look, and I took over to explain how she had shot Porter.

"It was undeniable self-defense," I said firmly. She had gone pale again when I spoke of it.

"No sane judge would deem it otherwise," Devons added. He looked away and whistled when Ward gave him a stern look. "Though of course I'm not at liberty to say such obvious things…"

I could have sworn I saw Ward roll his eyes. "That's enough for now, ladies. It's time for you to go home and get some rest." He let his gaze rest on me almost reproachfully. "As I seem to recall telling Miss Harper some hours ago."

I avoided his stare and focused on Felicity. "Will you be all right by yourself tonight? Would you like me to stay with you?"

She looked at us with great, despondent eyes. "If I can just make it home, I think…" She rose to her feet and wobbled. Devons instantly crossed to her and had her sit back down.

"My dear girl, do not trouble yourself!" He turned to Ward, expanding with chivalry. "Look at them, dear fellow! They mustn't walk home."

"I was going to call a ca——"

"Never fear, dears! You may stay with me, of course! I have a guest room just upstairs that my housekeeper keeps fresh at all times. Please give my poor heart a rest and don't make me worry about you going home alone tonight!"

I opened my mouth to assure him that I would be fine, but stopped, worried about Felicity. It wouldn't be proper for her to stay with him alone, and she wasn't in any shape to go home. Seeing me pause, he pressed on eagerly.

"Mrs. Johnson is still here; I could ask her to stay on for the night. She would be right next door to you, proper as can be."

I looked at Ward, who was considering him, looking torn between exasperation and resignation. He caught my eye and softened.

"She really shouldn't go out again," I said in a low voice.

He gestured to the door, and I followed him. "You'll be safe with Devons," he said quietly. "He's… overzealous in his hosting, but he's a good man." He stopped and glanced at the judge, bending over Felicity to refill her mug. His gaze moved back to me, and I realized he was worried. "I will admit I don't like the idea of you staying alone tonight, not when we haven't found Ragoczy's murderer. Yes, Porter is dead, and she was the one who seemed intent on killing you, but I'd like you to be extra careful for a while."

"Of course," I murmured. "I understand."

He paused, then withdrew something from inside his overcoat. "Since your knife was confiscated for evidence back at the Jacobses' house, I thought you could use this."

He unwrapped a small throwing knife with an ebony

handle and handed it to me. "I believe it will fit inside your boot."

I gave him a tiny smile, marveling that he had taken the time to replace my weapon, and wrapped it in the paper he gave me, placing it in the pocket of my robe since my boots were drying by the fire. When I looked up again, I realized we both had become very conscious of my informal garment, and neither of us knew what to say.

"Before you leave, old friend," called the judge, saving us, "do promise to come to breakfast tomorrow."

"I will," Ward said, and, tipping his hat to me, he opened the door and let himself out.

The rest of that night is a blur to me. Somehow I got Felicity and myself upstairs to the cozy guest room, which was papered in roses, and we fell into bed without undressing, slumbering deeply until the sun shone high through the lacy curtains.

When Ward arrived for tea, Mrs. Johnson bustled into our room without knocking, clucking her tongue over the state of us and providing us with dresses for the day. I have no idea how she managed to guess our sizes, but somehow the new dresses fit us, and where they needed a little tucking, she proceeded to tuck. She also brushed our hair, ignoring our protestations that we could do it for ourselves, and then bustled right back out, telling us in no uncertain terms that we were expected in the dining room.

I looked at Felicity; she looked at me, and without meaning to, we laughed. It felt good, after the trauma of the night before, and we found ourselves more light-hearted than I would have expected after only one night's sleep between us and the events of the previous day. Stomachs growling, we descended the stairs to the dining room and met Devons and Ward there. They stood as we entered, just as I remember the men in my family doing once upon a time. As we swished into our seats, our new garments rustling gently against the comfortable dining chairs, Devons beamed at us.

"You see, Tommy? Just what they needed. A good night's rest, my dears? Comfortable, were you?"

We nodded in tandem.

"Your house is just hotsy-totsy." Felicity twinkled at him. "I couldn't have slept better in my own bed."

"And I couldn't be more pleased. Do have some tea, my dear. Would you like one of these scones? Some eggs perhaps?"

I caught Ward's eye and looked away again, stifling a grin.

Ward cleared his throat. "Breakfast is not the ideal time for this, but I was wondering if you ladies would talk more about what happened yesterday. I'd like to hear from you —" he nodded to Felicity — "about the conversation you had with Ragoczy. I've heard Miss Harper's account, and I'd like yours as well."

As Felicity recounted the interview (word for word, but somehow without sounding like a parrot), Ward spread out pictures of the murder scene, studying them and taking notes on what she said, especially on pieces I had forgotten. Her recall was incredible to me: she remembered every bit of his office when Ward pressed for more detail. At one point, she was describing Ragoczy himself (more to show-off than anything, I thought with begrudging admiration), and she mentioned the ring he was wearing. I jumped, and Ward looked up.

"Ring?" he said.

"He *was* wearing a ring, wasn't he?" I tapped at my thigh and frowned. "But your pictures don't show him with one at the time of his death, do they?"

"No, they don't," Ward leaned forward ever so slightly. "Can you describe this ring?"

"Of course," Felicity said with a smug tilt to her mouth.

"It was gold, thick gold, and had a foreign language on it. I remember trying to read it when he was yammering on about truth being a construct." She rolled her eyes.

"And?" I pressed. "What did it say?"

"It was a foreign language, sweetie; didn't I just say that? At first I thought it said 'liberty,' but then I realized it didn't have a 'y'."

Ward's face was intent. "It didn't perhaps look like this, did it?" He flipped one photograph over and sketched a quick design on it. Felicity and I leaned forward to examine it.

It said, "Libertas in veritate."

The words were inscribed around a scale, similar to the kind one would use for weighing food.

"Yes, that's exactly it." She gave him a calculating look. "How did you know that?"

"I've run across it before."

She opened her mouth at the same time I did, likely for the same line of questioning, but he continued before either of us could speak.

"Miss Harper, I'd be happy to apprise you of the next steps of the investigation for the *Franklin* this afternoon. We've arrested Dr. Xavier for his part in the arsenic scheme, and I'm hoping to have a confession from him by lunchtime. Pritchard has done a nice job coaxing him to our side. He was considerably alarmed to hear that Ragoczy had died, even begging for protection. From whom, we haven't learned yet. But his reaction convinced several in the precinct who were inclined to see Ragoczy's death as an accident that it was indeed murder, and then we got the coroner's report, which confirmed the signs of a struggle. If you come by around..." he checked his watch, "three o'clock we should have a story for you."

"I'll plan to be there by three," I said, "but Ward, what does this mean? Is there... something... bigger out there?

Something to do with the symbol on that ring? Was Ragoczy reporting to someone else? What —?"

Besides the quick, piercing look he gave me, it seemed that he had heard none of my questions. He stood up from the table, shuffled all the photographs together, typed a note on his morsie, and gathered up the rest of his things.

"Thank you, ladies, and thank you, Arnold, for the breakfast. I must return to the station now. There are a few things I need to do."

"Wait," I said, standing too. "What is that design? How did you know it would be on his ring?"

"Please don't worry about it," he said, putting on his hat.

"Worry about it? Ward, what are you keeping from us?"

"I'm not going to tell you."

I followed him to the door. "You *have* to tell me," I said, my curiosity overcoming my politeness. "Why on earth wouldn't you?"

"I'm not going to lie to you," he said. "So I'm not going to say anything about it. Don't worry — you may find out in time." And again, he tipped his hat and left, leaving me staring after him, openmouthed.

A murmur came from the dining room, and then Felicity's bright tone followed.

"Isn't it just the most exciting mess? I went into the newspaper business for the pace, but if every case is like this, I might retire early! Not for the money, of course. Which reminds me, have you had any women sue for equal wages in your courtroom? I'd love to try it someday. It sounds just sensational, and the money couldn't hurt. But then Mac would probably fire me, so there's that."

I walked slowly back as she prattled on with Devons watching her. Even now, as I write this, I'd swear I saw stars in his eyes.

I slumped back in my seat and stared unseeing at the scone on my plate; triumph and confusion warred in my mind. We'd been right, we'd caught some culprits, we'd solved the Oak Hill poisoner case, but…

Some stories end with a bang, packaged nicely, all the loose ends wrapped tightly in a grim (or exultant) bow. But some stories end with a thump, and one emerges bruised, wondering where the rest of the story went after it tripped you and slithered out of your grasp. This story thumped, and I still feel bruised.

EPILOGUE

Thus ends my account of the Poisoner of Oak Hill. Ragoczy's papers proved his, Dr. Xavier's, and Gaines' guilt, and Sero Electric did indeed go bankrupt almost immediately, ironically paving the way for Panrose to become the leading electrical company in Luxity. I am reasonably certain that the Panrose hydroelectric generator will be the standard for electricity around the city within the decade. Xavier's license was revoked, and he was given a prison sentence. He could have had a shortened sentence in return for telling the police whom he feared so strongly and who might have killed Ragoczy, but he refused to do so until the day he was transferred to prison and was discovered dead, arsenic in his veins. Ward has not yet found his killer.

Before Felicity and I left his house, Brandtley gave me his harbor painting that rested over his credenza. When I hesitated to take it, he blanched, realizing that it could remind me of the attempt on my life. Seeing his consternation, I immediately accepted it, assuring him that I loved it just as much as I had before that night and that it would only remind me of his kindness. What I said was true, though I sometimes flash back to the night under the stars and its accompanying horror when I see it hanging by my mirror. I have decided it makes me stronger to face it every day, and I love it no less.

Ragoczy's murderer has not been found, though his nurse, Emmeline Porter, was found guilty of several murders of the past. Her death caused a collective sigh of relief from important, blackmailed people across Luxity, and I cannot honestly say I mourned her passing.

I have kept a careful watch on Felicity, but she has retained none of her earlier symptoms of grief or shock after she defended us from the attempt on our lives. Sometimes when we are working together, I remember with a jolt that I could be dead if she had not acted. I've wondered, too, what would have happened if I had gone home alone that night instead of letting Felicity take me to the water. Would Porter would have followed me home and killed me where no one could stop her? Perhaps I owe my underpaid assistant for every breath I take, and hence, every story I write. I can only thank God that I let her lead me to the docks when I wanted so badly to go home instead.

My shoulder healed nicely, and Ward's abdominal wound has as well. For this also I am thankful.

Two days after Ragoczy's murder, I met Diggory for breakfast, armed with an idea planted in my mind when I'd woken the day before. That morning I presented it to our circulation department, and they approved it. Diggory is the newest newspaper delivery boy for the *Franklin Journal*. He delivers all the newspapers that go to Oak Hill (whose *Franklin* circulation has increased since the poisoning), and he sees Chastity almost every day. On days I don't see him, I have Chastity's report to ease my mind that he is staying out of trouble — at least for most of the day. The money he earns provides for him and his sister, and I hope it will keep him from running with those who would do him no good.

Unfortunately, Edwin's and my brief meeting at tea was to be our last. He died the week after Ragoczy's death; his physician's treatment for arsenic came too late. The black bracelet around my wrist now has four strands for those who have gone before me in death: Nathaniel, Prudence, Gene, and now Edwin. Chastity looks as beautiful as ever in mourning colors, and I visit her faithfully to make sure she is recovering from her loss. She continues to hint at the man she'd like me to meet, but I have yet to give in to her nudges — or to attend any of her elegant parties.

Because of Edwin's death, Ragoczy's and Xavier's unresolved murders, and Ward's secretiveness, I repeat what I wrote at the beginning of this account: I cannot be satisfied with the ending of my tale. I wrote my story for the *Journal*, detailing what happened on Oak Hill and at West Hospital. Most of the headlines that I envisioned before going to the docks did indeed become headlines for the *Journal*. But I itch for more of the truth. Someday, and soon I hope, I will see the murderers brought to justice and the secret of Ragoczy's missing ring come to light.

I am Ginnie Harper, reporter for the *Franklin Journal*, and I long to reveal the truth above all else. So for now, I close this story, and I search on.

THANK YOU!

Thank you for reading the second of Ginnie's stories! Do you have a minute for feedback? Reviews help readers and authors: more reviews make books more visible so more readers can find them, (which means I get more support and can write more books), and thorough, honest reviews let me know what I'm doing well or what I need to improve!

Do you want to read more Ginnie Harper? Sign up for new book updates on www.britneydehnertbooks.com/ GinnieHarperSignUp! After you've done so, go to www.britneydehnertbooks.com/ginnie-harper-mysteries, and you can find behind-the-scenes goodies like historical references, deleted scenes, extra stories, and more!

BONUS CHAPTER

Keep reading to get a preview of the next book, *Truth in the Vault*....

THE TRUTH IN THE VAULT CHAPTER 1

My story started at the end of a blue-sky Monday after a long, boring week inching toward the end of winter. I was thankful for the lull in violent crime stories, as I was yet recovering from the shock of investigating the Poisoner. Ward was still speaking cryptically whenever I brought up the symbol on our poisoner's missing ring, and I found myself sulking during the grey days when he shrugged off my questions with the confidence of an experienced deflector of newspapermen. That winter was full of many things: petty theft stories; nightmares involving figures in black wresting me into dark, suffocating water; fits of helpless laughter over Felicity's antics; and drop-in tea visits to Judge Devon's house. I often was perplexed as to how we found ourselves there, and frequently Ward caught my eye with the tiniest hint of a grin before joining Felicity and Devon's banter. On this particular day, I'd just finished a story about the death of Corelli, one of the few remaining crime bosses in the City. He'd been poisoned shortly after my story about the Oak Hill Poisoner came out, making me wonder on particularly difficult nights if I'd given his assassin a *modus operandi*. It had been cyanide in his favorite wine, served by his step-daughter. Ward was still investigating the true culprit, but everyone in the City knew Feltz was behind it. It was enough to make me play Tchaikovsky with extra vehemence in the evenings. How does one cope with knowing the truth but being unable to prove it? Play the piano-miniature, of course. At any rate, though my mind had been busy with many things, I was beginning to itch for something new, a challenge to take my thoughts off the skulking of mobsters.

In this mood, I walked into Premier Bank on the southwest border of the City as I always did on the first Monday of the month to collect my meager wage. The bell over the mahogany door tinkled merrily, a sound I always found to be an odd contrast to the formal, somber air within. The teller at the first window in the peninsular desk nodded to me over the tray of coins he was sorting from the customer before me. I folded my hands in front of me over my pocketbook and breathed in the smell of leather, paper, and cigar smoke. The scent always transported me to my father's study, where I was expressly forbidden to go, but where I often went anyway while he was at work, especially in that dreadful last year after Nathaniel's death. When Chastity was practicing on the Grand piano and it was therefore unavailable to me, my fingers sought the keys of Father's typewriter for respite instead. Father often complained to the housekeeper about his dwindling supply of paper, but if any of the staff witnessed my misdeeds, they never betrayed me. Perhaps they sensed that without my music and my writing, madness was my only recourse.

"Miss Harper? I can help you over here." The friendly voice of the paying teller jolted me from my memories. "Ed will be engaged for some time. He's new."

Smiling at Ed, who was too engrossed to be chagrined, I stepped to the left where the dapper Jerry Johnson awaited me with a grin.

"I enjoyed your story about the new flower shop owner at

City Center," he confided, his eyes twinkling with mischief. I raised my eyebrows as I handed over my *Franklin* identification card so I could get my pay. He rolled his eyes at it and pushed it back.

"I seem to remember describing the owner as 'vivacious and compelling,' and her shop as 'a boon to flower-lovers and guilt-ridden beaus alike,'" I said. "Did you… perhaps go to find out for yourself?"

His grin threatened to push back the borders of his slick black hair. "I did indeed, I did indeed. We're both grateful enough to you that we agreed to give you this when you came in this month." He tapped the bills on the counter and then held out my money with an engraved card on top.

"Is this… a wedding invitation? Why, Jerry, I wrote that story only two months ago!"

"Seven weeks, to be precise." His tone reminded one of the smugness of a dog with a stolen bone. "We'd love to see you at the wedding in June."

Coins clicked in the background in Ed's counting tray. I laughed as I stowed my money in my pocketbook. "Are you putting it in the paper? I'd be happy to write it up for you."

"She did mention that, yes. I've only been engaged — briefly — once before, so I don't know the protocol."

A sly suspicion lit in the back of my brain. "Jerry… you didn't go to Elizabeth's shop as a repentant fiancé, did you?"

He winked at me. "A fellow never tells all his secrets. Let's just say I've moved onto greener pastures."

I shook my head and glanced behind me as the bell heralded another patron. "You and Elizabeth decide what you want in the article and send me the particulars. I wish you all the best. I'll take this," I waved the invitation, "and confirm that it's still happening before I come."

He shot me an aggrieved look as I edged around the other customer. "Doubting Miss Harper! I'll see you at the church in June!"

"Nice to meet you, Ed," I said as I passed the new teller on my way out. He managed a harried smile before attending to his counting machine.

Debating the odds of Jerry and Elizabeth's long-term relationship, I walked right into a young woman hurrying toward the bank.

"Oh! Terribly sorry," I said, patting my pockets out of habit. Nothing was missing, and the young woman flashed me an apologetic grimace, her magenta lipstick highlighting her full lips. Apparently too busy for words, she continued on into the bank, the door banging shut behind her with a forlorn tinkle of the bell.

Resolved to watch where I was going more carefully, I put aside the thoughts of the tangled banker-florist romance and focused on my next appointment. I was meeting Ward at the diner in fewer minutes than it would take to walk there; I accordingly made up the time difference by jogging. In that area of the City, no one gave a second glance to the rushed reporter in trousers and vest. Anticipating our diner conversation, I resolved not to ask Ward about Ragoczy's ring today: my questions had yielded nothing yet, no matter how cleverly I wove them into the conversation. I had yet to outmaneuver the smartest detective in the city — perhaps the smartest on the East Coast, I thought regretfully to myself, my optimism for getting information from him dwindling at the thought.

At least he would be paying for dinner, as he did two Mondays of the month: a raised eyebrow always accompanied any forgetful motion on my part to change the tradition. Any expression on his stoic face seemed more exaggerated than it would be on someone else, so a single eyebrow was enough to cause me to roll my eyes and withdraw my purse, secretly glad that it would remain the same weight when I left as when I came in. I was intelligent enough to notice that my turn to pay for our weekly debriefs somehow always came on the lunch hour at the cheaper venues. The fact that he accepted these meals was a boost to my self-esteem however, and the two times a policeman working with us hassled him about it, his disdainful glower brought about hasty silence and a rushed apology to me.

Contemplating the intricacies of my friend's personality carried me all the way to the diner, where, thanks to my daily exercise roaming the streets, I was barely puffing as I opened the door. Sinking gratefully into the well-worn cushions of our familiar booth, I imitated Jerry's smugness as I counted on one hand the times I'd arrived before Ward. Feigning nonchalance, I pretended to peruse the menu, which I had memorized and itemized in my brain in order of my taste preference.

When our favorite waitress had checked in twice, however, my smugness began to fade, and I instead felt the nigglings of worry. Finally, as I was checking my morsie for a nonexistent message from him, the door swung open, and he strode in, removing his hat with a nod to the cashier and making his way to our booth.

"East side," he said in response to the question on the tip of my tongue. "There was a shooting."

"Feltz?"

"One of his men," he replied grimly. "Or, boys, to be more precise. He's dead."

I winced. Even in this business, one never grew completely calloused to the death of the young — at least I didn't.

Studying Ward, I thought he didn't, either.

He ran a hand through his hair and drank the coffee our waitress handed him with murmured thanks. We gave her our order, and she traipsed off.

I thought of Diggory, our young street acquaintance who had saved my life back in the Blaster Murder days, and shuddered. For the millionth time, I breathed a word of thanks for his job as newspaper boy on Oak Hill where my sister Chastity could keep an eye on him — and where he was mostly out of touch with Feltz's men. The cheery noise of the diner filling my ears, I pushed back thoughts of him lying on a street somewhere, and instead pulled my notepad from my vest.

"Details?" I asked.

"Victim: about fifteen years old. Shooter: in custody. She's about five feet tall, in her mid-thirties, and has bobbed blonde hair. They were seen arguing in an alley before she turned the gun on him. She rifled through his pockets and took all his money — fifty dollars in bank notes — before fleeing. We caught her at the docks. Three eyewitnesses placed her at the murder."

I paused in my scribbling and studied him. "Any motive yet?"

"Not officially. From snippets that the witnesses heard, I suspect that she came after him because he murdered her boyfriend who was unable to pay off his debt to Feltz. It wouldn't be the first time."

"One wonders at her audacity," I said, tapping my pen on my leg. "Surely she knew Feltz would come after her next if you didn't find her first."

"Despair drives people to… extreme actions." Ward took another sip of coffee and dumped more cream into the swirling depths. "Often those actions are both self-detrimental and illogical."

I nodded, wondering again at the lengths to which some would go after a wound to the heart. Turning the question on myself like a mirror, I remembered that many would consider my actions after Nathaniel's death to be both illogical and self-detrimental: leaving a home and station of wealth and comfort to pursue the rigorous and, frankly, *shocking* career of a journalist. And not for a high society rag either! No, indeed. I had chosen the *Franklin*, of all papers. Instead of covering the events of the season or the galas celebrating Morislav's latest invention, I wandered Luxity on foot, dodging manure and crazed motorists to hunt murder, corruption, and mobsters. Most appalling of all, I spent my free time with a lowly detective, a mouthy journalist-in-training, and an odd judge who was secretly a painter. No wonder my family acted as though I had died. Except for Chastity: my heart warmed for my little sister, who was *still* trying to fix me up with a young, flivver-driving dandy on the Hill.

As the sunny waitress delivered our lunch with her usual flourish, I caught Ward furrowing his brow curiously at me and realized I'd been lost in thought for longer than was generally considered polite.

"Just thinking," I said lamely.

"She won't hang," he said, obviously surmising that my thoughts had been concern for the shooter.

"I'm afraid I wasn't pondering her fate."

He took a bite of his meal and settled back into the booth, scanning the room, as was his habit, before locking eyes with me again. I sighed.

"I was… thinking about how many would think my own actions were inadvisable back when I decided to become a reporter."

"Heartbreak-prompted?"

I flushed. "Well… it would appear that way, certainly. I know it was more than that: Justice-driven and all that. But… I won't deny that despair was part of it."

Ward nodded, his eyes drilling a hole in me. "One is thankful that you found a more productive means to work out that particular emotion."

I shrugged. "As I quite enjoy my life, I can say the same."

"What other stories are you writing this week?" He shoveled peas into his mouth with precision.

A sheepish grin crept across my face. "A wedding announcement, for one. I just finished the story on Corelli's demise this afternoon."

"I didn't think you did the wedding announcements." Mashed potatoes were the next to meet their swift dispatchment.

"Not usually." I forked a green bean and studied its floppiness with a critical eye. One of the prejudices that I'd unfortunately retained from my upbringing was an intolerance for overcooked vegetables. "This wedding is special." I couldn't help a laugh; I looked over to see Ward frozen with a piece of roast beef halfway to his mouth and looking distinctly alarmed. "I wrote a small piece about that new florist downtown a couple months ago——"

"I remember," he said with narrowed eyes.

"You do?" I was both taken aback and pleased. "Well, it turns out that the teller at my bank investigated her shop because of my story and found himself a fiancée." I sat back, enjoying the look of relieved bewilderment on his face. "It's awfully silly, but I'm rather tickled about it. They've invited me to their wedding." I gestured to the hand holding his fork in midair, and he registered a double-take before stuffing it in his mouth. "You're rather worked up for a wedding announcement. Someone you know getting married that you didn't want me to know about?" A thought struck me, and I eyed him suspiciously. "Are you… seeing someone?"

He choked. I almost offered to pat his back as he spasmed violently, but he regained control and rasped out with as much dignity as he could muster, "Heavens no."

"Well then," I said congenially, "what's there to worry about?"

"Nothing, clearly," he said, his eyes still watering. I handed him my handkerchief with a shake of my head.

"And you? What cases are you working this week?"

He leaned back and handed me my dampened hanky with another quick scan of the room. "There will be a few details to finish with the shooting, and I'm still investigating Corelli's poisoning."

I nodded, and he went on. "I need to ask Devons something about another ongoing case, something I'm not ready to talk about. It's…" he frowned.

"Unresolved?" I asked, thinking resentfully of the ring.

He quirked an eyebrow at me as if reading my thoughts. "Nebulous. Unclear. I'm not sure that it's even a case. I just have this inkling… a premonition, if you will, that it will become one. Too many related events."

"Coincidences?" I said innocently.

"I will tell you about the ring symbol when it is best for you to know: namely when I have enough information to make it worth your curiosity. There is no need to bait me."

"But detective," I said with something of Felicity's impish air, "baiting you is only ever a delight."

He chuckled and drained his coffee. "I think your partner is rubbing off on you."

"I wouldn't be at all surprised," I said meekly, finishing my soda. "Speaking of which, Devons has invited us to supper Friday. He said he'd invite you as well."

Ward nodded and leaned over the table as he pulled on his coat. "I will be there, as events allow."

"Crime never sleeps," I quoted.

"Hence both of our livelihoods," he pointed out, lending a hand to help me out of the booth.

I smiled sardonically. "Sadly, yes. Thank you." I glanced around the now-crowded diner and adjusted my own coat. The sky outside was darkening. "I'll see you Friday."

"I can walk you back," he offered, considering his watch and the street with a calculating eye.

"Chastity sent me home with her cook's best truffles," I said, guiding my hands into my gloves. "It's almost as if you knew."

He chuckled. "I will neither confirm nor deny that accusation. However, I *will* accept a truffle if you offer one."

"I'll see if any of the caramel ones are left," I said, feeling generous. "But I make no promises. You may have to make do with raspberry filling."

He paid the cashier, opened the door, and offered me his arm. When I took it, he positively trotted down the street with me in tow. "Come on, then. You're driving me to salivation."

My peal of laughter filled me with warmth from my smile to my sensible shoes.

ACKNOWLEDGMENTS

To Amanda, another slightly crazy chemistry professor like Dr. Laining, for fielding all my calls about MALDI-TOF MS's and spectrometry and water supply and poisons with infinite patience, thank you. You are not only a kind beta reader but also a pearl of a teacher to this poor, one-year-of-chemistry-in-high-school author.

To Clair, a real live reporter, thank you for your time and insight (aka brilliance) in answering my questions and correcting my ignorance. Ginnie, and her future series, owe a great debt to you. It was such a joy to find that there are reporters who, like Ginnie, have a passion for reporting the truth to the public. Thank you for your dedication and your stories.

To Amber, a star beta reader and fellow author whose critiques have filled in plot holes and tightened my writing considerably, thank you! I thank God for bringing us together on Instagram and therefore changing my author journey not just for good, but for much, much better. You are a blessing in many ways!

To Steve, for giving me a highly fascinating and very informative tour of the *Riverton Ranger*; thank you for helping breathe life into the setting of the fictional *Franklin Journal*.

To the Hive and its worker bees (including my former students!), thank you for your excellent London Fog rose tea and avocado toast. I wrote a large portion of this book on your very comfortable couch, and I'm grateful for your warm hospitality.

To my daughters, I know it is difficult when I write instead of playing "Dinosaur in Jail" or superheroes with you, and I want you to know that I love you with all my heart. I hope you will enjoy Ginnie and her stories when you are older. Thank you for being patient with your mama.

To my husband, who writes Ginnie's story plots and creates the concepts for these stories, the covers, and the titles: thank you for your commitment to our joint artistic endeavors. Thank you for supporting me in my passions and making time for me to write our books. You are more than I ever could have dreamed of when I thought about my future husband as a little girl! Thank you for being you.

To my parents and sister, my alpha beta readers of everything I write, from children's books to poetry to mystery to fantasy: thank you. This journey would not have continued without you. Your encouragement has meant the world to me over the past five years. To Mumsie: I wrote this book with glee, knowing that you would enjoy it far more than the fantasy series you endure for your daughter's sake. Ginnie is for you.

ABOUT THE AUTHOR

Britney Dehnert is a writer, poet, teacher, and mom. A lover of character-driven stories and writing in general, she's half of the creative team behind the Ginnie Harper Mysteries, the Epoch Mythos series, and the Dark Moon trilogy. The other half is her husband, J.P., who brainstorms with her, plots and outlines the stories, deals with her veering off his outlines, and creates covers and fan fun. Britney and J.P. make their home wherever they happen to be at the moment with their two daughters. They love road trips (where they come up with their best ideas together), epic blanket forts, picnics in the living room, exploration from the backyard to distant planets, wardrobes that lead to fantasy lands, and, of course, golden doodles.

You can read more from them on their website, www. britneydehnertbooks.com/sneakpeeks

ALSO BY BRITNEY DEHNERT

GINNIE HARPER STATICPUNK MYSTERIES

The Truth in the Dark

The Truth in the Water

The Truth in the Vault

Epoch Mythos Series (for Fantasy fans)

Journey of the Maple

Anchor Between Worlds

See www.britneydehnertbooks.com for all books and blog posts by Britney Dehnert.

3e5386a1-476d-4b02-8c91-902c0d53953bR01